FALSE HOPE

by Meli Raine

She thinks she's fooled me. But I've known all along.

Almost.

Lily is hiding something, a secret so big, she came out of a year-long coma and her first instinct was to *lie.*

Who does that? Someone who is afraid. No—not afraid.

Terrified. And it's my job to take that fear away.

My partner and I have spent countless man-hours hunting down the cold-blooded killer who did this to her. Meanwhile, Lily's spent her waking hours recovering. Getting stronger. Getting smarter.

Staying beautiful.

Never get involved emotionally. That's my dictate. Never get attached.

When you realize you're caught in a triangle, it turns out there is no exit.

Crossing a line is easy. Holding a line takes strength.

Lily's shooter knows that she's my weakness.

And he's about to exploit that by breaking a line and escaping, claiming a hostage in the process.

One I have to get back.

No matter what it takes.

Listen to the audiobook, narrated by Audie award winner Sebastian York!

CHAPTER 1

*I*f unicorns had a flavor, it would taste like kissing Lily. Her essence is still on the tip of my tongue as I watch the layered response Lily has mastered. Observe her as that beautiful mind works to line all the pieces up and execute the subterfuge, living in two selves, one ever vigilant, one struggling to stay quiet.

For months now, I've felt it. *Sensed* it.

Now I can taste it, too. Lies have a flavor.

And God help me, I want more of the deliciousness of Lily.

But those lies come with an aftertaste, a bitter acrimony that has an overriding power.

My own words ring in the air like a gong as I wait: *When were you going to tell me you've been faking the amnesia, Lily? Before or after I sleep with you?*

"Sleep with me?" she squeaks, the words catching me off guard. I assumed she'd deny the lying.

Not talk about my fantasies.

"You want to talk about *that?*" I choke out, amused and sickened. "You've been lying to me for close to a year and all you want to talk about is sleeping with me?"

"You brought it up!"

She's got me there.

"How about this fake amnesia bullshit, Lily? How about we

1

talk about *that* before we discuss getting sweet between the sheets?"

She blushes.

I get hard.

This—*this* is why I should have recused myself from this damned assignment long ago. I knew this day would come. I knew I'd have to call her on the lying.

Worse than that—I knew I wouldn't be able to help myself.

One kiss. Then another. Then my hands all over her.

And then more.

She's torn. I see it. I'm giving her everything she wants—the freedom to tell the truth. Nothing feels better than that when you're trapped.

Not even a great kiss.

Unless you're a sociopath—or worse—holding a lie for too long is its own torture. Imprisoning yourself is harder than being controlled by outside forces. Duality is inherently draining. How can we be whole and centered when our very survival relies on being split and vigilant?

The lies in her eyes are breaking my heart. Before she even says a word, I know she's about to snow me. That's where she's at now. That's who she *is* now.

A liar who lies to stay alive.

Can you blame her?

And for what I'm about to say to her—*do* to her—can you blame *me*?

The blush in her cheeks matches the emotion pouring out in her breathless, rapid breathing. Lily still hasn't answered my question.

She hasn't answered my question because when you lie, you buy as much time as possible.

"Lily?" I ask her, as if the prompt is necessary. We both know it isn't. It's a formality.

But it's a formality that matters.

"I—I—" she mutters, shaking so hard, the blood draining out of her face and pooling at the base of her neck. The flush along the V of her top turns a bright red like a sunburn, a slap, a memory.

Her body remembers.

And Lily is fighting her body. Fighting all the pieces of herself that tell her the lie is the only way to survive.

"From the way you're acting," I point out, "it's pretty clear. From the moment you opened your eyes, you were lying. You've been lying all along."

I push her with a look. I don't need touch. I don't need force. All I need is a tone. She'll take the accusation and convert it into shame.

I'm just the catalyst. She does all the work for me.

This is what makes guys like me different from the rest of the world. We're trained in psychological techniques that you're not supposed to know even exist. We use them, in stealth mode, a verbal judo where we turn your weaknesses against you and conserve our strength.

Lily squares her shoulders. A shaky breath comes out of her.

"Why do you think I'm lying?" she asks.

More stalling.

"I'm not going to tell you why I think it," I shoot back. "I'm going to tell you that I *know* it."

Wide eyes meet mine, her eyelids fixed, her expression half dazed, half panicked. "I told you everything I know. Everything I remember about the shooting."

"Except for one little detail, Lily. You forgot to mention that you know who the shooter was."

"I swear, Duff. I swear," she says in a voice that begs me to believe her. "I swear I told you everything I know." Her fingers fly to her mouth, the tips of her index and middle fingers brushing against lips I just kissed.

I can take a lot in the line of duty. My tolerance is sky high. What I didn't know until now is that I can't handle being lied to by a woman who just kissed me like her entire life depended on it.

"Who are you protecting?" I demand.

"Protecting?"

"Yes, *protecting*. The only reason you won't cough up a name is because you're protecting someone. Who are you working for?"

"You think I'm working *for* someone?"

"Yes."

"You think I'm a *spy*? One of you?" Her shaky hand moves, arm outstretched, index finger pointing at me like an accuser at a witch trial.

"I'm not a spy."

She snorts. "You're not *not* a spy."

"You're avoiding my question, Lily."

"Which is?"

"Why have you been lying since the moment you regained consciousness?"

Rapid blinking is a sign of stress. Stress is a signal that someone is lying. Lying is a strategy used to get your own way.

Being lied to by a woman I've come to admire and want desperately makes me want to blink, too.

I don't.

I don't because I'm well trained. Then again, no one trained me for this scenario: how to handle falling for a client. The only "training" we received on that was one word:

Don't.

The car lurches, swerving slightly. Mike's doing a great job as driver. The barrier between the front and back seats is thin and although the glass is smoky, I know Mike saw that kiss. Kiss*es*. Plural kisses that will come back to haunt me if I don't construct a damn good cover story for why I'm making out in the backseat with a client who was just nearly murdered in cold blood in a coffee shop by a guy pretending to be a gang member.

"I don't have an answer," she says.

Finally.

A little honesty.

"You do," I contradict her, my own voice going gentle. Anger permeated everything I said after that kiss, a kiss that was hotter than I even imagined. For the last few months, every fantasy I've

4

had has involved kissing her. Lily's innocence and pain is at the forefront of what I want to soothe.

What I never anticipated was her heat. Her *passion*. That underneath the strong, determined woman I've been shadowing these last nine months, there was a fully formed, full-fledged being with needs. Wants.

Desires.

And the way she kissed me back tells me she wants me, too.

What the hell am I supposed to do with that when she's looking me in the eye and *lying*?

"What's my answer?" she challenges.

This verbal ping-pong game is killing me.

"You know who tried to kill you at your parents' shop nearly two years ago. You're not telling anyone because you're terrified."

She doesn't move a single muscle.

Doesn't breathe, either.

"I need to know *why* you're terrified," I press.

The change in her expression is extraordinary. I've done it. Mission accomplished. By moving the conversation from *who* to *why*, I've cracked open the steel drum of Lily.

She sighs.

Palms up, I give her my best *I'm on your side* look and say, "I don't need to know *who*. Not yet."

The suspicious look she gives me is well deserved. She knows I'm bullshitting. That's fine.

It's just a step.

"But I need to know *why*, Lily."

"Why?"

"Why what?"

"Why do you need to know?"

Aha. Pay dirt.

"Because it's critical to saving you." I run my fingertip along a line of dried blood on the back of her hand. "If you don't trust me, then this is going to continue."

"Is that a threat?"

The chill in her voice gives me goosebumps. Damn. I've radically miscalculated her.

Who is manipulating whom?

"Why would you ever think I would threaten you?" I ask her, unable to keep the emotion out of my voice.

Unable to keep my emotions out of my blood as well.

In this business, we don't get surprised very often.

But Lily's surprising me—left, right, and upside down.

"You're telling me that if I don't trust you, then people are going to continue trying to kill me," she says through gritted teeth, snatching her hand away.

Intensity isn't generally one of Lily's character traits. Right now, I'm seeing parts of her that I didn't know were in there.

My bad.

I've radically underestimated her, and now I'm going to pay the price.

"That's not what I meant," I protest. I hate being defensive.

It's my own fault I'm here, though.

"Then say what you mean," she demands.

The defensiveness fades, my training kicking in. I have to think of her as a client and not as someone I just kissed.

"Has it occurred to you that the reason people are shooting at you is *because* you're lying to everyone?"

Her face goes pale.

More pay dirt.

I've hit a nerve. Causing her pain is the last thing I want. On the other hand, if causing her pain keeps her alive, then bring it on.

Even if it feels slimy and cheap.

"I'm not lying," she shouts, the sound bouncing off the barrier between us and Mike. Any doubt he hears everything is long gone.

"Yet you're not telling the truth."

"Why did you just kiss me?" she demands.

The question should rattle me more than it does. Some part of me is prepared for it, knowing she's just deflecting.

"Because I knew it would be the fastest way to get the information out of you."

Her mouth trembles. It tightens, the skin around her eyes going soft, emotional, filled with betrayal. Embarrassment.

Hurt.

I can feel her thoughts. They echo in my mind. Learning how to read someone means taking on their emotions. Doing it in a calculated way to analyze what you need to know in order to act means keeping your distance.

Kissing her violated that rule.

"Then that kiss was just part of work." Her question isn't a question. It's a knife through my heart.

A heart that's not supposed to exist right now.

I shrug. "Think what you want."

"That's not what I *want* to think," she grinds out, her voice going low and hard.

"And I don't *want* to think you're a liar who's been stringing me along for the last nine months, either, Lily. I don't *want* to think that you can't trust me. I don't *want* to think that you've been putting your own life in jeopardy, your parents' lives in jeopardy—hell, even Bowie and Gwennie. I don't *want* to think that you've been deceiving every single person on your security and medical team for all this time. So it looks like we both have things that we don't *want* to think about."

"It's not like that," she protests.

"Then what is it like?"

When people are really close to cracking, they develop a vibration. It almost has a scent. I can feel it radiate off the subject.

The subject.

Sounds brutal, doesn't it? She's a twenty-five-year-old woman who experienced a traumatic brain injury when someone shot her in the back of the head, from behind, in a case of mistaken identity. I'm falling for her, a slow burn that I keep trying to extinguish, the embers roaring to flame before I can catch my breath.

And here I am calling her *the subject.*

Reduce a human being down to a single word. And then take what you need from them.

That's my job.

Lily is my job.

She can't be anything more.

But if I don't get this right, she becomes something *less*.

"Why are you so afraid?" I ask again, moving towards her, letting my muscles go loose at the same time they gear up to protect. She inhales slowly, watching me as she judges, taking in information to form a conclusion. As long as her eyes stay on me, she can analyze whatever she needs to process her decision.

Decisions.

I know she's making plenty of them about me.

The car comes to a complete stop. I look up. We are at a small airport, parked behind the building. Gentian's here, with Jane, the door cracked open. Mike gets out and leaves us alone, the car stifling as it idles, oblivious to the drama unfolding within its doors.

"We're alone now," I assure her. "No one's listening. No one's watching."

"How do I know that?" she asks. "For all I know, I'm being bugged."

"I told you, you're not."

"Then why did someone try to shoot me and Jane the minute we started to talk about—" She cuts her words off.

"Talk about who?" I ask her.

"Talk about that day," she says, eyes unfocused. She's breathing through her mouth and trying to regulate herself. It's damn hard to do that when you're recovering from a brain injury. But somehow, Lily manages.

Lily *always* manages.

"We were talking about that day," she says slowly, remembering. "The day I was shot. And then suddenly the bullets started flying." Her eyes met mine, pleading with me to make it okay to tell more.

"Someone must have a listening device on me," she continues, "because the minute we started talking about hi–" her words cut out again. I swear the word she was about to say was *him*.

"You know exactly who tried to kill you, don't you, Lily?" I ask, my voice barely a whisper. Frustration makes me want to shout. Instead, I go quiet.

Calmness can be more unsettling than direct confrontation.

"Who are you *really* working for?" she demands, changing the subject. Pivots like this don't work on me. She doesn't know that. "It's not Drew Foster, and it's not Silas Gentian." She takes a few breaths. She waits.

I let the silence yawn between us.

"I work for Drew," I finally reply.

"And?"

"And *what*?"

"And who else? Who's your real boss?"

"Who's yours?" I ask.

"Mine?" Her voice goes up, high and reedy, surprised by the question. "I don't work for anyone, Duff. I'm just what you see. I'm just a twenty-five-year-old woman who was working in her parents' flower shop when some guy came in and *shot* me in the back of the head. I'm not the one here who's pretending to be someone other than who I am. Who's your *real* boss?"

I can't answer that question. I can't for many reasons, most of them reasons she suspects.

But here's my real problem: my actual boss is dead.

I'm not sure who I'm working for anymore.

My paychecks come from Drew Foster's company, but my *orders*?

Those came from someone who isn't in charge now. Never will be again, either.

So whose agenda am I following?

And what if it turns out—it's my own?

CHAPTER 2

*L*ily looks over at the building, turning to the left and seeing the small aircraft on the tarmac. A pilot is climbing into a helicopter. "I thought you said we were meeting President Bosworth," she snaps. Her voice is filled with confusion, the kind that comes from being overwhelmed.

"We are."

Frowning, her eyes dart all over the place, inside the car, outside the car, frantic and worried. "Isn't he here in California? It was all over the news. Why do we need to be at an airport for a helicopter?"

I tell her, choosing to go into asshole mode. "Security. And speed. But before we go, you need to tell me, Lily: Why are you so afraid to tell the truth?"

"Maybe I just don't trust you."

"Will you tell the truth to Gentian? To Jane?" I counter.

Her reaction confirms what I already suspect.

No.

"Jesus Christ, Lily," I say, moving my hand to my forehead, rubbing hard. Two parts of me are fighting for dominance inside. I'm not sure which one is supposed to win, and the battle is epic.

No—pyrrhic. No matter what, the half that loses is the half

that will hurt the most. And no amount of victory for the other part will balance that out.

"Is there *anyone* you trust?" I finally ask her. This is the end of the line. Whatever has her in a state of terror so great that she can keep this kind of secret for this long under extraordinary brain-trauma circumstances, it's got to be bad.

Imperceptibly, she shakes her head. I pick up on it. It's so faint, like seeing a butterfly flapping its wings and noticing that it's out of sync for just a heartbeat.

"What about your mom and dad?" I probe.

She lets out a huff, a strangely cynical reaction that sets me on alert.

Tap, tap, tap.

We both look up to find my boss, Silas Gentian, standing outside the car giving me a look that says, *Why are you delaying?*

I thought we were going separately, but I guess President Bosworth changed the plan. We're flying together. Makes the gravity of this situation feel stronger.

Lily crosses her arms over her chest, folding her shoulders in. The position is one of protectiveness. The fact that she has to protect herself against *me* makes this even more frustrating.

I roll the window down an inch.

"What's going on?" Gentian asks, eyes bouncing between the two of us, brow low with irritation. "Bosworth's waiting."

"I know," I tell him. "Lily was just telling me some vital information about the case."

"Which case?" Gentian demands. "The shooting that just happened or the one from two years ago?"

I look at Lily. "That's a really good question, isn't it?"

She says nothing.

Gentian rolls his eyes, jaw going tight. "We don't have time for this kind of bullshit," he snaps. This isn't in his nature. Lots of security guys mistake anger for authority. Gentian is not one of them. The fact that his girlfriend was just targeted along with my client in the shooting back at the coffee shop certainly feeds into whatever is going on inside him.

Again, we're not robots.

11

Even if we're told that's our *real* job.

"I don't have anything new to add," Lily pipes up. Pleading eyes meet mine, begging me not to blow her secrets. How the hell I could do that when she hasn't even told me those secrets is a whole other issue, but I get her meaning.

Don't push.

Don't make her go places she's not ready to go.

Gentian has his own calculations going on. All these competing interests fly around the space between the three of us like atoms in an electron microscope.

It's Lily who breaks first.

Reaching for the door handle, she pops it open, shoving so hard that Gentian jumps, his hand reflexively moving towards his gun. "Fine," she says, the single word a slap across the face, a kick in the gut, invective.

Gentian and I scramble to keep up with her. It's only because I'm walking behind her that I can detect her limp. It's more pronounced. Back at that coffee shop, she didn't take a bullet.

But she did take a beating.

I catch up to her quickly and walk side by side, turning and surveying her body.

"How badly injured are you?" I ask, brushing her shoulder with my hand.

She flinches and pulls away, yanking with a force that makes a part of me cringe. "I'm fine. I told you, I'm *fine*," she insists.

"Just because you say it doesn't make it true."

"Now the things I *do* tell you are lies? I thought I was only lying by omission, according to you." The bitterness in her tone makes me want to turn back the clock.

Makes me wish I'd never kissed her. Makes me wish I'd been able to kiss her differently. Makes me wish we'd met under completely different circumstances.

Makes me wish for a lot of things.

But wishes aren't reality. What's in front of our faces is the fact that someone tried to kill her and Jane. They set it up to look like a gang-revenge shooting.

Now I know that they did it at the exact moment that Jane

and Lily were talking about the shooting from almost two years ago. No one on my team is bugging her. No one is bugging Jane.

Or at least not in the way that Lily thinks.

It's obvious, though, that *someone* is listening. Monitoring these women. But there's no way that shooting was set up knowing they'd talk like that.

Jane swallows Lily in a hug. As the door of the building shuts behind us, Gentian leans over to me with a conspirator's whisper.

"What were you trying to get out of her?" he asks quietly.

"You know exactly what I was trying to get out of her," I reply, giving him a look that says he's a an asshole for asking when he knows the answer. "What we've been trying to get out of her for the last nine months."

"Do you really think she remembers anything new?" Gentian asks, incredulity infusing his words.

He has to ask that question. I understand he has to. And quite frankly, I don't know how to answer it.

"I think she knows more than she's letting on," I reply.

"Czaky has been claiming she knows. That the right neurologists and psychologists can get the information out of her. That's been his fucking mission ever since she woke up."

Gentian's words slice through me. I know it's true. Romeo Czaky's been working hard on the case, determined to find the person who tried to kill Lily.

But there's something in Gentian's tone this time that sets my teeth on edge.

Maybe it's the combination with Lily's reaction earlier. Maybe it's the combination of that and trying to be two different people inside my head at the same time for so long. Maybe it's the way Jane and Lily are talking, whispering furiously to each other.

Maybe it's everything.

Maybe it's nothing.

"Czaky's been obsessed with this for a long time," I reply, stalling.

Doesn't work on Gentian.

"That's a non-answer and you know it, Duff," he says, looking at me even more intensely. "What the hell are you hiding?"

I laugh, the sound quick, like a bark. What does he mean, hiding? My feelings for Lily? My actual mission? Pick one, Gentian.

"I'm an open fucking book, and you know it."

"You're also a liar."

"That's why you pay me the big bucks, boss."

His turn to laugh, except it doesn't sound funny.

"What do you make of this mess?" he asks, his voice going quiet, the timbre digging into the base of my spine. I know that voice. It's the voice that lives inside my head every time I think that a client is in more danger than I had previously suspected.

Hearing it in my boss does not strike a note of confidence.

"Someone set that whole thing up long before Jane and Lily were talking," I say.

Scrutinizing me with a look that only someone with a long history of being shot at can give, Gentian rolls his tongue inside his cheek and stares me down. I stare back. No one needs to train us in staring techniques.

It comes with the territory.

"You're not going to tell me what you know," he says, voice firm. Decisive. As if it's not even worth his time and attention to try to argue with me.

I shrug. That's all I need to do.

"Goddammit, Duff," he says, betraying himself. "That's my girlfriend they shot at today. That's my girlfriend they tried to kill two years ago. That's the goddamn president of the United States' daughter."

"*Illegitimate* daughter," I remind him.

"That doesn't make any of this better," he grinds out.

"No, sir. It doesn't. Makes it worse."

"Bosworth is losing his shit behind the scenes," Gentian confides in me. "I've got Drew freaking out, too. His wife just had a baby. And now the president's *other* daughter gets shot at. My *girlfriend*."

"It's a big mess," I say, sympathizing.

"It's more than that and you know it," he answers. "This reeks of an inside job."

I swallow hard, relieved that *he* said it.

Not me.

"I agree," I finally spit out, the admission setting my nerves on edge.

In our business, you don't admit what you know, unless it furthers your cause. Every scrap of information is a tool. Leverage is more important than reality. But times like this require a certain candor. I'm not laying all my cards on the table, but I'm going to show a couple of the ones in my hand.

I have to. Because those gunmen weren't just shooting at Jane. At the president's daughter.

They were shooting at my client.

They were shooting at my *Lily*.

We are interrupted by our driver, Mike, who turns to Gentian and says, "Chopper's ready." The guy looks like every invisible agent you could possibly imagine. Dark hair. Short haircut. Sunglasses, even at night. Black suit. Burgundy tie. Concealed weapons. Always—*concealed* weapons.

"Destination confirmed?" Gentian asks him.

The guy just nods.

"Everything's cleared," Gentian says to me. There's a bleakness in the way he says it. It's as if we're about to cross an enormous gap. But that line was crossed hours ago by the guys who chose to open fire in a residential neighborhood and shatter store windows in a joint designed to caffeinate—not kill.

Silas's phone buzzes. He looks at it and grimaces.

"Dammit," he says, pivoting to hit the wall hard with the heel of his hand. "Jake's dead."

I go cold. The guy on detail at the coffee shop, front and center when those bastards opened fire from the car.

"Son of a bitch," I mutter under my breath. "He take any of them down?" I ask, knowing it doesn't matter in the long run. Doesn't matter when he's dead.

And yet it does.

15

"Preliminary reports say he tried to take out the tires. Shot out the back window before they got him in the head."

The cold, clinical way that Gentian tells me this is another way that we hold our distance.

An image of a bullet ripping through Lily's face bursts into my mind suddenly. Any illusion that I have distance here is long gone.

This is a first.

It has to be the last.

Jane appears, marching over with Lily in tow. The chopper on the tarmac starts up, the early sounds of the engine turning over like a hacking cough from a virus no one wants to contract. The blades even out and soon it's just a whirr, one I know all too well. Combat, supply missions, civilian life, behind-the-scenes politics—you name it, I've done it in a helicopter.

But I've never transported an injured client I just *kissed*.

"Ready?" Jane shouts to Silas, who takes her arm and strides with her to the chopper, Lily behind them, me on her heels. She looks straight ahead, the blade's push of air getting stronger, blowing her hair off her face. The scar from her gunshot is revealed, a winding mess that makes me fall for her a little more, nudged forward into territory I have no right to explore.

We recover from our wounds because the survival instinct is so strong.

And those who survive and thrive are the most attractive of all.

CHAPTER 3

The ride to the undisclosed location is devoid of drama. Just the way I like it.

When you're buzzing like a mosquito above the Southern California coastline, conversation isn't a priority. Lily's sitting next to Jane, across from me and Gentian. The second we land, she unclicks her harness, twisting away from me.

I get it.

I'm the enemy now.

Telling the truth makes people hate you.

Demanding *they* tell the truth makes people want to kill you. No one wants to be reminded that their very existence depends on someone who can see through their lies.

And there are two types of people like that: narcissists, and people who really do have something to lose.

I know Lily doesn't have a character disorder.

Whatever she's worried about losing must be bad.

"Here," I say to Lily, pointing to the car.

"Why are we in a car? Can't we just land at the president's house?"

"Security issue."

Everyone loads into a standard black sedan, big enough to hold a driver and the four of us. I sit in the front. That's what I do. There is no discussion about who sits where.

Lily, Jane, and Silas climb into the back, Jane between the other two. No one says a word.

We are a strangely well-oiled machine, pieces that come together to work in sync. We don't do this because of orders. We don't do this because of some weird psychic connection or premonition.

We do it because this is the way survival works. This is the way *intelligence* works. Not the kind of intelligence that all human beings possess. The kind of intelligence that involves research behind the scenes, in the shadows, in the nooks and crannies where political animals live and thrive.

In some way I don't understand, Lily has learned to speak our language. She's vigilant. *Constantly* vigilant, with the dual understanding that everything she does has to be done surreptitiously, and at the same time, that she has to be aware of every single movement, every word, every signal that every person in a given setting is sending out.

We turn into receivers. We take in radio signals and interpret them. We spit the results back out.

That's how it has to be.

That's how we're made.

The jerky drive through the streets surrounding President Bosworth's personal compound changes the minute we make a certain right turn. Down a slope to a garage where the doors don't open the way they do in the civilian world. This is where we'll enter the Byzantine maze that will take us to a room where Jane will find herself standing in front of a man who looks at her with eyes that tell a thousand different stories and absolutely none —all at the same time.

When you have eyes like that, you get to lead nations.

If we were in civilian life, Lily would be shaking by now. Normal nervousness requires an identification with other people as social beings. We get nervous when we think we might be excluded from the social group that we need in order to stay alive.

Exclusion is a tool. Expulsion is a weapon.

There's a reason why shame is used so often as a tool to

control other people. Shame disconnects us from the social group. That disconnection can lead to death.

But here's the key: you can climb awfully high or live awfully low if you don't care about the shame.

It takes a lot to reach that point.

But once you do, the nerves—they learn something exquisite. They learn to simmer down, to settle in, to curl up and just watch the way the world moves and unfolds before them. The nerves learn that they don't have to react or anticipate in the same way that they do when you actually care what other people think.

I can tell by the way Lily moves that she's gone beyond the point of caring.

That's a shift I didn't expect in her.

You can't work in a florist shop, giving people bouquets of happiness, arrangements of sorrow, blossoms attached to emotion, and not care. Then again, Lily changed almost two years ago.

Where did she go for fourteen months inside her own head?

She's still changing, before my very eyes.

It's the little things that make me realize she's different. There are no questions on this ride. She doesn't ask where we're going. Or why. It's the lack of *why* that gets to me more than anything else.

She knows that President Bosworth is Jane's father. No one else knows that outside of the circle of security people who surround the president.

Who now surround Jane.

My phone buzzes and I look down. It's a text from Gentian, who's sitting right behind me.

How is Lily really? the text asks.

I stare at my own glass screen and almost make a sound that reveals that my nerves aren't quite as flat as I thought.

You know more than I do, boss, I text back.

He immediately responds with, *Bullshit.*

Holding my face neutral, I reply, *She was close to telling me something.*

His reply is a simple, *Get her to talk.*

Trying, I type back.

Try harder, he replies.

And then the question that I know is coming but don't want to read:

What do you think she knows?

No clue, I reply.

Does she know who her shooter was? he texts.

Don't know, I reply.

What else could be so important that she'd hide it? Silas writes.

I need time with her alone, I text back and then another text comes through.

It's from Lily.

Quit talking about me when I'm sitting right here, she texts. An aggravated sigh ripples up from the back seat, crossing over the headrests, sinking into my ear.

Silas and Jane start whispering furiously. Another text comes in from Lily: *My mom and dad want to know when I'm going to get home.*

We'll take care of that, I text her back. *You okay?* I add at the end, the question stupid and vapid. I know it's an empty social nicety. Funny how those pop up whether you like it or not. Just when you think you've driven them out of yourself, it turns out social conditioning is a hell of a lot more ingrained than anyone ever imagines.

F-I-N-E, she texts back, complete with a poop emoji.

The car halts, tires screeching on painted concrete. I snap my door open. Gentian does the same behind me and we're out.

Walking down a hallway, long, bright fluorescent lights blinking like a cliché, we walk to double metal doors that open as if on command. Everything here is electronic, on lockdown, controlled by computer chips and humans watching security cameras, their eyes less reliable than the algorithms built into the systems.

And yet, they are our last line of defense.

The need for human beings is both greater and less in our line of work. As technology takes over more of the menial steps, the irony is that it's in some of the most mundane work that we find deeper truths.

Evidence is all about human error.

Justice is as much about the smallest mistake as it is about the biggest reckonings.

We walk quickly down yet another hallway, taking a sharp right, the doors blurring like road signs on a highway, flashing past until nothing can be read. I look down to see Lily's calf, the fabric torn around the cut that goes down into the Achilles tendon.

The blood is dry. The wound is superficial.

But it's a reminder of my failure, yet again.

That scar on the back of her skull is an indictment.

The fake gang shooting that just took place at the coffee shop is testimony that our systems are less foolproof than we thought.

This isn't a game.

Not when lives are at stake. It *is* a strange sort of competition, though. The goal is to win. The goal is to stay alive. At least that's how it works on our end. The other side has different goals. Goals that remain hidden.

But the ends are oddly the same.

We stop in front of a nondescript door. That's also part of the point of all of this. Nothing stands out, especially us. The door opens and Gentian walks in, followed by Jane, with Lily right behind her. Reaching the doorway, I look in over her shoulder to see President Bosworth attempting to hug his daughter, who freezes in place, clearly awkward.

And then it's Lily's turn to freeze in place as her eyes turn to the left and I spot the object of her gaze.

It's Romeo Czaky.

Of course he's here.

Lily squares her shoulders and takes a long time to inhale. The strands of her new hair brush against her shoulders. I ache to reach out and touch the long, curling ends, the locks carrying a meaning I don't really understand right now.

Her whole body tenses, moving with a jerky quality. It reminds me of the early days when she was learning to walk again. When she would have seizures that left a part of her body connected to the rest, but unable to do its job.

I lean forward and whisper, "You okay?" into her ear.

"Quit asking me that," she mutters, her voice cold and dark.

A chill starts at the base of my spine and works its way up and down at the same time, spreading like a fast-growing vine that seeks every spot of light it can suck up in order to build and spread and strengthen.

Something about her words, combined with the way she's pointedly not looking at Czaky, tells me before her mouth ever opens what she's been hiding from me all along.

I get it now.

And it's so much worse than I ever imagined.

CHAPTER 4

e move into the room and arrange ourselves around a small round table. Unlike every other meeting like this, I make sure to sit down next to Lily. I position us so that she's not anywhere near Czaky. Jane, too, avoids him. I brace myself. I get it.

I've missed what's been in front of my face the whole time.

Impossible.

Impossible. There's no fucking way that Czaky is involved in the shooting. How could my own partner have been the shooter?

I'm jumping to conclusions that I have no evidence to support. It's just gut instinct now.

And that's another hard part about this business.

You go with your gut a hell of a lot more often than you go on hard evidence.

The president has his own private security team, Secret Service on standby, two of them in the room watching everything.

The chain of command is obvious. So is the pecking order in this room. I'm the lowest of the low. At least I'm right there with Czaky.

"Gentian," says the president. He looks at me. "McDuff." Then he looks over at Romeo. "You both know Czaky. He's working security with me now."

"You're Secret Service now?" Gentian asks Romeo.

"No," the president answers. "Romeo's leading it. Privately."

A ripple travels through the air in the room like a breath pushed out too fast, like water swallowed in a bolus that sticks in your throat, unable to move in either direction, causing pain and discomfort, an obstacle that you just have to ride out until you can figure out the way through.

"Congratulations," Gentian says in a calm, even voice that I know damn well I need to emulate within the next two to three seconds.

I grunt in Romeo's general direction, "Good job."

Lily looks down at her hands, splayed against the tabletop. Jane makes a strange, strangled sound that would have meant something else a few minutes ago.

Now I understand *exactly* what it means.

How could I have been so stupid?

"I know all of you know each other," President Bosworth says as he looks around the room. "And I know everyone here except for you," he says, looking and speaking directly at Lily.

"But of course I know who you are." His smile almost reaches his eyes. If it went all the way, I'd be able to see his resemblance to Jane. Remaining cold, he looks nothing like her.

Lily looks right back at him, swallowing hard but maintaining her composure. "And obviously I know who you are, sir," she says, with a nod of her head, more wry than her usual demeanor.

President Bosworth lets out a laugh. It's a chuckle that recognizes the last two years. Two years since his life blew up. Two years since his own wife, Monica, tried to kill him. The event made international news, especially when it all shook out, the truth of Monica Bosworth's deception and involvement in dirty political games that led to bloodshed and worse.

Somehow though, Harwell Bosworth, the senior senator from California, made it all the way to the White House in a contentious election that no one really expected him to win.

But he did.

My grandmother used to say that in the end, after nuclear

war and pestilence, after Revelation and the world coming to an end, the only thing left would be the cockroaches. As I look at Harry Bosworth from across the table, a man I can only refer to as *Mr. President* or *sir*, I see that cockroaches come in all shapes and sizes.

"You're obviously both fine," Mr. President says, looking at Jane and Lily for confirmation.

Jane gives him no quarter. Lily just nods.

Fine, I think to myself. That's right. They're both just *fine*.

The president turns to Gentian and asks, "Any idea who did this?"

A curt nod followed by a head shake from Gentian. "No, sir. We have our suspicions."

It takes everything in me not to look up at Czaky.

Lily tenses as Jane turns to her father and says, "Do *you* know who did it?"

The president seems to expect the question. He gives a nonchalant shrug, one almost designed to piss her off. I know immediately that there's a good chance that the guy *does* know.

"No idea," he says.

That's the right answer, of course. We don't give information in this job. Not even to our daughters.

"Even if you knew, you wouldn't tell me," she says, her bluntness appealing.

Like Lily, she's been through hell and back.

That prickly feeling takes over along the edges of my spine. There's something else Jane and Lily share. Czaky was with Jane the night she was assaulted by Nolan Corning, President Bosworth's biggest enemy.

The day that Lily was shot at the florist shop, Czaky was there, too.

How the hell did Czaky work his way up to the president's personal security team? He's not Secret Service, so this is deep-state shit. There's no way Drew Foster is providing Czaky's services to the president directly. A million questions race through my mind.

I can't ask these questions, though. Can't probe. Can't dig.

I'm just a grunt.

At least, it's my job to make them all think that.

So far, so good.

"Excuse me, but why are we here?" Lily asks the president, her head tilted in a way that is so innocent. She expects a direct answer. That's the part that's so naïve.

"You're here to be debriefed," he says, looking at her head on, reading her. He looks away quickly, dismissing her. To him, she's just a distraction.

I wonder, too, why we're here. If he wanted a meeting with Jane, wouldn't he just ask for that?

"Lily," the president says, leaning forward, "do you remember anything new?"

Czaky's face is blank. *Too* blank.

That tingling sensation takes over my body, but I don't show even one neuron's worth of activity on the surface. My body must be self-contained and under complete control at all times. Any hint that I see that Czaky has moved up into echelons of power that give him leverage against Lily is a death sentence for her.

The complexity of her ongoing silence unfolds, layer by layer, inside me. I want to reach out and put my hand on hers. I want to wrap my arms around her. I want to be a shield. The enormity of what she's holding inside her rolls out like an algae bloom taking over.

She's right.

She's been right all along not to trust anyone.

Including me. Czaky's partner.

The room is pregnant with expectation as the president stares at Lily, clearly expecting a response. You don't get to that level of power and ask a question and *not* get an answer.

"No, sir. I don't remember anything about what happened the day I was shot. At least, not the part where I was shot." Her voice warbles a little, filled with the kind of nervousness that you expect in someone who is normal.

And by normal, I mean part of the masses. Someone who

isn't in the security field like me, like Czaky, like Gentian. Someone who actually cares what other people think.

Her performance is masterful. It's a performance, though. Make no mistake about that. So far, the president seems to be completely snowed by it. An imperceptible tilt of the head, the president turning towards Czaky, makes me realize that they're closer than I ever imagined.

I look at Lily with even more admiration.

Because her instincts are dead on.

Whatever she knows will get her killed.

How deep does Czaky go? How involved is President Bosworth? Did *he* order the hit on Jane? Would a man hire a hitman to kill his own daughter?

Maybe.

Maybe if she's illegitimate and her very existence threatens his ability to become president of the United States.

That would be a great theory if it weren't for one pesky little detail: Jane is still alive.

A determined, cold-blooded man on the rise to the White House would have had his hired help finish the job. Jane was a target for reasons that aren't important to Bosworth. Might never have even been on his radar in the first place.

Which means Monica Bosworth is the one who hired the hit on Jane.

Romeo came to The Thorn Poke nearly two years ago to kill Jane, on Monica's orders. Then Monica died, shot to death to defend then-senator Bosworth. Their daughter, Lindsay, threw herself in front of Harry to save his life, even after she learned he wasn't her biological father.

Even with her own mother's gun pointed at her.

My mind is nothing but threads, all weaving together, the pattern ugly but starting to emerge as a whole, a picture, a snapshot.

One I don't like.

Czaky was there in the sex club the night Silas and Jane were attacked.

27

Czaky calls Bee and Tom regularly to pump them for information under the guise of *caring*.

Czaky was there the day I found the poisonous spider on Lily's arm.

Czaky was there the day Lily was shot.

Czaky was there at The Thorn Poke and rushed into the store... with a red rose petal stuck to the bottom of his shoe.

Why does that matter? Because there were no red roses in the front of the store that day. The shipment had come into the back. Which means he tracked that petal in from the back of the store by... racing around to rescue Lily from the front.

That detail has stuck with me these two years, unanchored to anything else.

And there's one more detail I don't like:

Czaky is now on the president's personal, off-the-record security detail. Who is pulling this guy's strings now that Monica is gone?

"Isn't anyone going to say something?" President Bosworth demands, the silence after Lily's words eating away at the thin veneer of civility.

"What do you want to hear?" Romeo asks. "Lily answered you. Do you believe her?"

Silas gives me a sharp look, eyes moving, face staying still. *Don't argue*, those eyes say. Meanwhile, my legs tense, quads and hamstrings ready to leap. To lunge.

To take down.

"Why wouldn't I believe her?" Bosworth asks, turning to Romeo with a puzzled look.

Because she's lying, I think but cannot say.

Will not say.

Ever.

CHAPTER 5

"I asked Romeo to be here," President Bosworth says, leaning forward and spreading his arms out on the conference table. It's a power play, one that's beneath him.

You don't need to position your body like a silverback gorilla when you're already head of the band. It makes him look weak. He doesn't seem to realize it, but Gentian gives me a look that says he caught it, too.

"I assumed that having him here would help all of you," the president continues, as if we're all supposed to be grateful.

It's Jane who allows her face to move, eyebrows shooting up. "You thought having Romeo here would help us in a way that having Silas or Duff here doesn't?" she asks, her voice halting and curious.

"Romeo and Duff were the only ones present at the shooting," Bosworth says to her, his eyes narrowing, features going soft, as if remembering the horror that didn't materialize. "They're the closest thing we have to eyewitnesses."

Lily blinks exactly once.

"That's right," Romeo says, standing. He sticks his left hand in his pants pocket, turns, and walks two or three steps before pivoting and giving me a standard bureaucrat's granite face. "It was you and me, Duff." He frowns, his mouth pursing slightly. "Actually, *you* were the first one on the scene."

"We've been through countless meetings about this," I say slowly. "What's new here today?"

If you watch Lily at the level of detail that I'm trained for, you can see she's struggling. If you pay attention to every single breath she takes, you see how much internal glue she's using to keep herself from falling apart.

I'm pretty sure Romeo sees it, too.

But here's the part he doesn't know–all that effort she's putting forth has to do with him. With protecting herself and her family from him. And that glue? That glue is part of a completely different system inside her.

One that he can't possibly understand.

Guys like him never have someone worth protecting. It's a force they simply don't understand.

It's a lack of understanding that comes from living a life without an anchor.

It is their weakness.

"Sir," I say to President Bosworth, standing and giving him a soldier's posture as well as a grunt's level of respectful attention. "If you'd like me removed from Lily's detail, I absolutely will recuse myself." I look at Czaky. "I'm done with this bullshit."

The use of profanity makes Silas clench his hands. In an informal setting, he wouldn't care.

But this *is* the president of the United States, after all.

Jane laughs. Lily blushes. Bosworth just stares at me. "Why would an innocent man recuse himself from her detail?" he asks, eyebrows going up, the question pointed.

I just stare back.

And wait.

"This is all a distraction," Romeo breaks in. "A convenient one." His eyes go to Lily. "I understand you are remembering more and more."

"Says who?" she challenges him. "Who told you that? You've become a creepy stalker who keeps following me, bothering my family, calling my mom and dad." She starts to rant. "It's like you're making things up just to have some reason to slither your way into my life."

If I thought the president's eyebrows were raised with my use of the word bullshit, I had no idea how high they could *really* go.

Until now.

Lily's words clearly catch him off guard. She's on the attack, standing and walking behind Jane's chair, moving close to Romeo to get a good eyeful. Her posture is aggressive. Challenging.

In charge.

"My mom keeps telling me I'm supposed to remember more because *you* keep calling her and telling her that I should be remembering more. My dad had a heart attack while *you* were there, pushing to interrogate me when I had barely come out of my coma. My little sister tells me that *you* go to her high school and offer her and her friends rides home, and that most of them don't accept. But Gwennie does sometimes. And when Gwennie *does* accept your creepy ride home, all you do is pump her for information about *me*."

Lily looks at President Bosworth. "Maybe he's just doing that work for you?" Her voice goes up, the question like a burn. "Maybe he's just doing his job?" she asks, giving Silas a similar look. "But all it feels like is a creeper coming along when I'm disabled and barely finding my way back to living after some asshole decided that he had the right to take my life. I don't care that he thought I was Jane. Jane doesn't care that he thought I was Jane. None of that matters. What matters," she says, her finger out, pointing directly at the president of the United States, "is that the head of your security team is creeping on my fifteen-year-old little sister, weaseling his way into my life, all because he's convinced that I remember a traumatic event that I have no way of remembering because I was shot in the back of my fu–my *head*."

Her fingertips go to the edges of her lips. "Pardon the profanity, Mr. President." Pink cheeks and lowered eyes make it clear she's really embarrassed.

The room is filled with nothing but the sound of our collective breaths. No one is in sync. It's a cacophony of hushed sounds as we wait to see what the president says.

Slowly, hawk-like, he turns and looks at his head of security. "Czaky," he says, his tongue moving to the edge of his mouth, rolling slightly into a tight ball, "you pick her little sister up from high school and give her rides home?"

"Sir, I've taken her mother to the dry cleaners to pick up suits for funerals before. I've even purchased tampons for female clients. You know how this job is. We do whatever it takes to get the information that we need. To serve our mission."

"And your mission includes my little sister?" Lily pipes up.

"Your little sister is part of your family. Your family is at the center of one of the biggest violent mysteries in modern politics. And you weren't there," Romeo says, taking one step closer to Lily.

She doesn't flinch.

I nearly do.

"You weren't *there*," he repeats, "to watch your brother and sister cry their eyes out every night while your parents slept by your bedside in that hospital." He starts to shake with emotion.

Too bad it's all manufactured.

"You weren't *there*, Miss Lily, when Bee wailed and sobbed in your father's arms, while I got cups of coffee to keep them going through the night. You weren't *there* for the thousands of man-hours that I put into this case to make absolutely sure that Jane, the president's daughter, was as safe as possible from the corrupt network of people who somehow made a decision that she needed to be annihilated."

Jane bristles at the mention of her name.

"And you weren't *there*," Czaky says, looking at me, "the day that I saved her from Nolan Corning. So, sir," he says, turning back to Bosworth, "yes, I gave a fifteen-year-old girl rides home from high school to her house, or to The Thorn Poke, so that her parents didn't have to spend as much energy worrying about her as they did about the daughter who was shot in the back of the head in a case of mistaken identity, where the killer was trying to kill—" His words cut off as he looks at Jane, standing over her, their eyes connected in a creepy dance.

"To kill the daughter of the president of the United States."

CHAPTER 6

A slow clap, sickening in its mockery, greets his words after a few beats. It's a cleansing sound, like hitting reboot after a computer crashes.

"You're right. I wasn't there. Except I was." Lily's mouth curls up in a snarl. "I was there, in the room, in a coma. I was there, on the bed. I was *there*. Maybe I was nothing but a surface to *you*," she spits out. "An assemblage of pieces of meat kept alive by blood pumped through me. My breath had to come from a motorized machine, but by God, I was *there*."

Jane reaches for Lily's hand in a gesture of support.

Lily snatches her fingers away.

"Don't you dare lecture me about who was there!" she shouts at Romeo. The two Secret Service agents exchange glances. Shuffling sounds in the hall make it clear the president's other guards are deciding what to do next. Romeo looks up and gives them some kind of signal through the glass panel.

They back away.

"You don't care about me, or my mom and dad, or my brother and sister. You care about your mission, don't you?" Pure, righteous glory radiates out of her. It's blinding.

So blinding, President Bosworth narrows his eyes.

"And you, sir," she says to him. "Were you the one who directed Romeo's mission?"

Pandemonium kicks off, the sound of Romeo shouting at Silas, of Bosworth's now-chief of staff, Marshall Josephs, coming into the room. The blond ex-basketball player is a formidable opponent in an argument. He's got a soft paunch and a hard face. In seconds, he assesses the room, takes a seat next to the president, and whispers in his ear.

Bosworth freezes.

Then looks right at me.

"Who do you really work for, Duff? My son-in-law tells me you're a bit of a chimera." Drew's his son-in-law, not Marshall, so whatever the man just hissed in Bosworth's ear has come through quite a few people in the network.

"I'm not fictional, sir." I pinch the skin on the back of my hand and hold it up. "See?"

He doesn't laugh. "You joined the firm with a background that's pretty extraordinary. Sent into combat at eighteen. A kill number that raises eyebrows. Military intelligence and then you disappear off the map for seven years."

I just stare at him.

He's right.

"And now you've been working for Drew for three years. You're the quiet guy who might as well be a curtain panel. You fade into the woodwork perfectly."

"Thank you."

This time, he does laugh. "You knew that was a compliment. Good. But here's the rest: you have a mission within a mission. It's becoming increasingly obvious."

"Sir, we all have a mission within a mission unless we're Secret Service." I look at Romeo. And even then...

Silas squirms in his seat.

I just told a truth I shouldn't have.

But it's one we all know.

Lily is still waiting for a direct answer to her question to the president. He doesn't look like he has any intention of responding. He's fixated on me, for reasons I don't understand. I look at Romeo.

Then again, maybe I do understand.

"I have no mission other than protecting Lily and other clients who sign on with Drew Foster's company," I say, laying it all out. "I watched Jane before Lily, and clients I could name with permission before Jane. My job is to be a grunt, sir. I make sure people's hearts keep beating."

"Then we have very similar jobs, Mr. McDuff," the president says to me.

"You have about three hundred and twenty-five million more clients than I do, sir."

That gets me a sarcastic curl of the lip.

"Who ordered someone to kill Jane?" Lily asks, cutting through the bullshit in the room.

Jane looks up at her, gratitude in her eyes for making her a priority again. At the same time, there's a rueful look on Jane's face. She knows that there will be no answer to Lily's question. She knows that there *is* an answer.

It's just not coming out right now.

"I don't know," the president lies.

I know it's a lie because if anyone knows, he does. He may not know who the killer is, but he knows who hired the killer.

My blood runs cold. Lily's words echo through me.

Were you the one who directed Romeo's mission?

What if she didn't mean picking up Gwennie, inserting himself into the Thornton family's lives?

What if she was asking the president of the United States if he ordered a hit on his own daughter?

"The mess involving my wife," Bosworth starts, his voice halting as a pained expression pinches the corners of his eyes. "My wife was involved not just in the scandal that you read about in the newspaper, Lily. She had connections going back decades to some rather unsavory characters in government and in narco trafficking."

Nothing he's telling us is anything we haven't read about in the news or seen in documentaries thrown together quickly by production companies looking to make a dollar. But Lily takes it all in with a wide-eyed absorption that makes a part of me ache on her behalf.

"Do you really think that Duff was part of it?" she asks Bosworth, leaning towards him with an earnestness that only a naïve young woman could have.

I look at her and then I look at Jane. They're the same age. Before the shooting, Lily did look just like Jane, at least from behind. That's what the killer thought. And as long as he got the target, the mission was complete.

Is that what's going on? He needs to complete the mission? Except Lily was never the intended target. Jane was.

Which one was the target today?

President Bosworth watches me for the few seconds it takes to process all of this. Without looking at Lily, he addresses her question. "I don't know who is involved in what. Part of the problem, Lily, is that when you've been in politics long enough, everything gets blurred." His tone changes to one of wistful nostalgia that sounds brutally fake to my ears. "People betray you," he continues, "and they save you." He smiles sadly. "They go behind your back and they dig knives into your shoulder blades. Hopefully a metaphorical knife in the back, but sometimes a real one, or a bullet or," he gestures to her, "worse, what happened to you. I'm so sorry you had fourteen months of your life taken away by an act that was intended for someone else."

He looks at Jane.

Silas goes tense.

"You were both there," the president says to me, then Romeo. "Duff was closer. Romeo was seconds behind, from what the report says. Of course, you, Lily–and you, Jane, were there as well. It's only you four who know what really happened."

"And the fifth," Lily adds. "Don't forget the fifth person in all of this."

I force myself to keep my eyes on Bosworth and not look at Romeo.

This situation has become a strange math equation. When does five equal four? Apparently it does now. But that's the kind of math that makes me suspicious. Men in Bosworth's role don't make mistakes like that.

Marshall whispers in the president's ear, sliding a piece of paper across to him. It's half written on, with extremely slanted, almost horizontal cursive in the margins. "We have other meetings to attend, sir," he says to Bosworth with a raised eyebrow. "You're already late."

Bosworth looks at Lily. "You really have no more memories?"

"No, sir."

He looks at me. "And no new evidence?"

"No, sir," I echo. He doesn't ask Romeo the same question.

Turning to Silas, the president gives him a meaningful look. "What are you doing to prevent another shooter from trying to kill my daughter?"

"Everything in my power, sir," Silas says.

It's a standard answer. It's what everyone wants to hear.

Best of all, it's true.

"This does not look good," Bosworth says to Silas.

Marshall nods, a short, staccato movement. Bosworth catches it, face filled with chagrin.

"It's not public knowledge yet that Jane's my daughter. We need to keep it that way," Bosworth says, glancing at Lily, who nods.

"Of course not, sir," she says. "I would never say a word."

"But if it did get out there, it would be even worse, knowing that someone is trying to kill her again," Bosworth says, looking up at Romeo. "Maybe I should assign you to cover Jane."

"Sir," Silas says, his voice firm. "I've already got it covered."

"You had it covered today, and look what happened," Bosworth says, his arm going out in a gesture that seems to point to me.

"Harry," Silas says, breaking protocol and calling the president by his first name. "We lost a man out there. This was designed to look like a gang shooting. It was a set up. It wasn't a mistake on our part."

"I don't give a shit whose mistake it was or what kind of set up it looks like, the bottom line is that my daughter almost *died* yet again today. Lily almost died again today, and all of this is somehow connected to the mess Monica created and left for me." He stares Silas down. "Fix it."

"It's not that simple."

"I don't care how simple or how hard it is. *Fix it.* That's your job, and if you can't fix it, I'll find people who can."

Romeo smirks at me as he, Bosworth, and Marshall file out of the room.

I reach for Lily's shoulder. She's shaking.

"Well, that was fun," Jane says under her breath.

"You and I have a different idea of fun," Lily says.

Jane snorts.

"Is he always like that?" she asks, beseeching Jane with a look that says *Please tell me no*.

"Are *you* always like that?" Jane replies, giving Lily a once-over that says she's re-evaluating her. "That was one hell of a speech."

"What speech?"

"The way you talked to Romeo. Good for you."

"What do you mean, good for me? I was just trying to tell the truth. The guy's a jerk and then he's accusing Duff, like it's Duff's fault that I got shot."

"He had a point," Silas says.

All of us turn and look at him. But I'm the one he's looking at. "You were there. You think I don't know that?" Our eyes meet.

He's feeling me out.

"Of course I know you know that. Bosworth's going to evaluate that when he's looking at the whole situation. I know you've already examined my role. Romeo appeared out of nowhere during the shift change at the flower shop and he came in time to help. That's all I know."

Lily studies me like she knows I'm lying.

I look back at her.

That makes two of us.

"Do people really suspect Duff?" Jane asks, looking at Silas like his face will reveal the truth.

He shrugs. "People suspect everyone. That's how this game works."

There's that word again: game.

Except this time it's a false game and it's all based on a false memory.

But here's the deeper issue: As Lily walks out of the room ahead of me, I watch the way her hair rests against the nape of her neck. How she moves, just slowly enough as she sets pressure on her right foot, to make me remember how injured she was.

Here's the other issue: that kiss.

I *should* be worried about Romeo pointing the finger at me. I *should* be worried about Bosworth interrogating me. I *should* be worried about the shooter randomly targeting people and setting everything up to be fake. I *should* be focused on my job. And I am.

That kiss—that kiss was part of my job.

But it was also part of *me*.

Bosworth and Romeo are worried about memories. Lily's running around like she has no memories, or worse–*false* memories.

And me?

What if it turns out I'm just living with false hope?

CHAPTER 7

The ride home is long and cold, like the air changed after a freak rainstorm. The kind you expect to cleanse and renew but instead it leaves messy yards, hail damage on cars, and flooding that wreaks havoc.

Silas took Jane home in a separate vehicle. I'm taking Lily wherever she wants to go. She's so quiet, the hug goodbye from Jane lingering in the way she holds her body. Her limbs look like they've given up. Like everything good in the world is long gone.

Her stillness is a problem.

Lily is the epitome of movement. All those long months in that hospital bed were an anomaly.

"You want me off your detail?" I ask again, making sure she understands I'm not the enemy as we drive in the direction of her house. I shrugged off Mike, the driver assigned to us. It took some arguing, but once we got to the outer gate of the president's private home, this place they call The Grove, I won.

"I should."

"Do you?"

"No. I trust you more than Romeo."

"That's not saying much."

"Good of you to realize that."

"Are we going to talk about that kiss?"

"What kiss?"

She makes me laugh. Only Lily could make me laugh at a moment like this.

A part of me feels like I should apologize. I don't. Apologizing could make her think that I'm taking back the intention.

And that's the last thing I want.

That kiss was full of crystal-clear purpose. The lingering question is: was her purpose the same as mine?

"Do you really think I might be working for someone?" she asks. I pull the car over to the curb, leaving the engine idling. "You know I'm not a spy. I don't do what you guys do."

"I know."

"Then why would you question it?" she asks.

"Because we have to. That's how it works. And because of what happened to Gentian."

"What happened to Silas?"

I know Jane knows what happened to her boyfriend's fiancée, but sitting here in the car, I realize Lily has no idea. Is it worth breaking confidentiality to explain that the man fell in love with a woman who turned out to be a double agent?

That he had to kill his own fiancée in the line of duty to save high-ranking government officials?

The thought freezes me. Not much sends me into a state of paralysis, but this does. For a split second I am Silas Gentian. I am staring at the woman I've fallen for. I am holding a gun to her head. I am pulling the trigger in order to save other lives.

How did he do it?

How does *anyone* do it?

As Lily stares at me, how does she entertain the thought that I'm the one who held a gun to her head? Who pulled the trigger?

Then again, how could she *not*?

"Duff? What happened to Silas?" she asks again.

"He had to kill his own fiancée in the line of duty when she turned out to be a double agent–maybe triple–and started assassinating government officials on an air strip."

Her mouth drops to an O of shock.

"I had no idea!"

"It's not like he wrote about it in his annual Christmas letter."

"But–does Jane know?"

"Of course."

"How–how awful! How do you do that? How do you kill someone you love out of–"

"Duty? Doing our job? What we do, Lily, is not much more than protect meat bags and weed through mind fucks."

Wide eyes meet mine. "Could you explain what you mean by that?"

I point at her. "You. You're a meat bag–"

"WHAT?" She looks stricken.

"So am I. We're all just organs tied together with bones and tendons and flesh, with blood pumping through us. My job is to make sure that blood keeps pumping through you. That's the simple part."

She frowns, still confused.

I sigh and continue. This is a lot of explanation, but it's important. "At its most basic core, that is what I do. But then there's the mind fuck. The psychology and strategy behind how we make sure that we protect you. In your case, someone is trying to kill you. How do we discern motives? How do we figure out which places are safe? How do we determine how involved you are in the plot to kill you?"

"Me? Why would I be involved in a plot to kill *me*?"

"Are we being manipulated? Are we manipulating? These are all questions that are part of what I do for a living. Same as Silas and Drew. This is what I'm trained for, Lily. I'm just a grunt. You're coming into it as a civilian and as a traumatic brain injury survivor."

She frowns. I trudge on. "So yeah, you *should* look at me with suspicion. And that's okay. I'm not offended by it. In fact, I would think the other guys weren't doing their job if they didn't take into account the fact that maybe I *did* try to kill you."

Our eyes meet on that last sentence, exactly the way I planned it. I know I didn't hold that gun to her head. Trust is a funny thing. It requires that you let go of a certain part of humanity inside you. We have to override our instincts in order to trust because instinct says that survival is more important than connection.

But connection is how you survive. How do you let go of what is programmed into your DNA in order to *save* your DNA?

That's the great conundrum of being human.

That's exactly why Lily is dangerous for me.

"Tell me more about you," she says, propping her feet up on the dashboard and giving me a weird mixture of an interested smile and a distasteful demand.

"What about me? I'm Duff. Seamus McDuff. Thirty-four years old. Army combat vet. That's all you need to know."

"I know you like coffee. Really good coffee."

"Yes. What else?"

"Where are you from?"

"Philly."

"And your parents are there? Brothers? Sisters?"

"I've got one brother. Parents are dead. Raised by my Gran."

"What's your brother's name?"

A hole opens in my chest. "Wyatt."

"Where does he live?"

"Don't know."

"What do you mean, you don't know? I know where Gwennie and Bowie are."

"Gwennie and Bowie are kids."

"Of course they're kids. How old is Wyatt?"

I do quick math. "Twenty-seven."

"How do you not know where your brother is?" Her face changes as the answer dawns on her. "Oh, does he do what you do for a living, too? Is he, like, deep undercover in some motor-cycle gang?"

I laugh. "Way to stereotype, Lily."

"Well, it's real, right? I mean, I watch it on *Sons of Anarchy*. You watch that show?"

"Sure."

"Mom loves it."

"I can't imagine Bee getting into that kind of violent enter-tainment."

"Oh, no. She doesn't watch it for the violence. She watches for the nudity."

Now I know she's pulling my leg. I laugh.

"You think I'm joking? You've clearly never admired Charlie Hunnam's ass."

"Got me there."

Her turn to giggle.

Here's the other thing about trust: I have to give her something. That's the only way I'll get her to confide in me, but that means I have to trust her. What I give her can't be fake. It has to be real. So far, so good, because my little brother really *is* missing. And no, he's not in the field.

He just went missing.

And it was my fault.

"How old were you when your parents died?"

Pain stabs me in the temple, memory rising up like a spire to the heavens. "Eleven."

She gasps. "So young!"

"Right."

"You don't want to talk about it, do you?"

"No."

"Okay, then—where did you go to college?" she asks.

"I didn't. I ended up in Afghanistan."

"Were all of you there? Jane said that Silas was there."

"Yeah. I was there, Silas, Drew, Drew's friend Mark."

"Were you there at the same time?"

"No. I didn't know any of them over there."

"What was it like?"

"What do you mean, what was it like? It was a hellhole. All combat missions are hellholes."

"Fair enough. When did you go?"

"When I was eighteen."

"Eighteen? I'm trying to imagine Bowie being in the army and going through basic training and being sent off to Afghanistan in a couple of months. He's seventeen and his idea of discomfort is when he can't get two double cheeseburgers at a fast-food restaurant."

"Yeah. I noticed."

She laughs. Then she stops, abruptly. "Tell me, Duff. Tell me the truth. Who *can* I trust?"

"You can trust me, Lily."

"Isn't that exactly what a killer would say to someone he was trying to convince?"

"Yes. You tell me, Lily. Why'd you go after Romeo today?"

The pulse at her neck flutters, giving away her emotional state even if her face is a blank slate. "What do you mean, 'go after'?"

"You went off on him."

"Yeah. I did. He was being a jerk. I'm tired of letting people be jerks."

"You did it in front of the president of the United States. Romeo is the head of his private security. That took some guts."

"Maybe I was just being stupid and emotional and got overwhelmed."

"I don't think that's it, Lily. I don't think you got stupid or emotional or overwhelmed. I think that was calculated."

She shuts down. I watch it, piece by piece, like emotional origami as she folds herself back in.

"I want to go–" she cuts off her words. "Wait. No. I can't. I can't go home."

"Why not?"

"Because someone's trying to shoot at me. I don't want to take that kind of danger and bring it home to Mom and Bowie and Gwennie and Dad."

"We've already figured it out. We've got a place for you if you want it."

"You do?"

"Yeah."

"Mom's going to freak when she finds this out."

"She already did."

"You talked to her?"

"Yeah. She wants to talk to you."

"Oh, God," she groans. In some ways, Lily's just a normal

twenty-something woman and in other ways, she's ripping my heart out. "What's this place that you have for me?"

"It's a secured location."

"What does that mean?"

"It's a safe house."

"What's a safe house?"

"It's a place that's been checked over for bugs, for safety issues."

"Sounds like a prison." I shrug. "I don't want to go there."

"You don't want to go home. You don't want to go to the safe house. Where do you want to go?"

"I want to go home with you."

CHAPTER 8

*I*t's cold.

That's the first sign that something's not right.

It doesn't get this cold out here, where the sand gets between your toes and stays there for eighteen months, like it or not. Wind whips against the sides of my tent, rattling them until they sound like the banshees that my Irish grandmother used to tell me about.

She warned me they were real. That they came to haunt bad little boys. I always thought that was a crock of shit.

Maybe Gran was right.

I roll over and realize that what I thought was my sleeping bag turns out to be wet and slick. There's fur on the top, above the part that sticks to me. I reach down in a panic and find myself holding a tongue.

Not a human one, either.

And it's attached to something.

Sitting up on my cot, I am in a pool of mud, the tongue gone but the breath still hot. Mud squishes between my toes, pushing the sand away. I'm naked, I'm cold, but I'm not alone.

An inner vibration takes over my spine, shaking me until the tremors make it impossible to stand up. Vulnerable and completely unarmed, I assess my situation in a half-asleep state and realize that I'm fucked.

The tent flaps are making a horrible whacking sound, as if someone is taking a hammer and hitting as hard as they can against the tent poles. The fabric ribbons out and forms a strange melody with the wind. Creatures start to run around in the muck and mire around my legs.

I look down, but suddenly the space is dark. There's no moonlight. The creatures crawl up and down my arms, the viscous wet and dank smell of the mud turning to a copper tang I know too well. I'm coated in blood and now, finally, I can stand.

Stumbling through the dark, I find the corner of the tent. I'm disoriented and have no idea which direction is north, but I know that I've found an edge.

A boundary.

A beginning.

"Duff," calls a voice in the distance. It's not my buddy. Not my commander.

It's Lily.

"Help," she cries out, her voice filled with pain.

Panic does strange things to our circulatory systems. The heart starts to beat faster and harder. Blood pumps into the arms and legs to ready for fleeing or fighting.

Unfortunately, that means the blood doesn't go to the brain in the amounts that are needed to be able to think through a layered strategy.

This is why we make mistakes when we panic. Because our brains literally can't work right.

As I fumble along the edge of the tent, my hands find the canvas, dry and clean. I move foot by foot across the edge, seeking a door, an exit, a way out to find Lily. As I hit what appears to be a split in the fabric, I reach for the opening and find another solid surface.

This time it's cold. Smooth.

Bone.

"Where are you, Lily?" I call out. The wind whips into my ear so hard. I pull back, stuck between two worlds: the unknown, bleeding sand and the known, muddy horror.

"Where are you?" she screams.

That's it. I step out. I'm drawn by a force I don't understand, unraveling second by second. I may be naked and covered in blood or mud or whatever this is, but I know this.

I have a mission.

To save her.

I take exactly three steps and crash into a similar-sized being. His body is radiating heat and he smells like a bear.

A very pissed-off, angry bear.

"You can't have her," the bear says to me, his fur coated in blood. "She's mine."

Instinct makes me shove as hard as possible, until the bear splits into a thousand black birds. They flock around me, nipping with their beaks, cawing into my ear, the sound a mourner's wail.

"Help, Duff!" Lily calls out again, telling me that the bear hasn't killed her yet.

I run towards the sound of her voice, slipping and twisting, feeling something pop in my ankle but ignoring it. We're trained to do that. Ignore everything but the mission.

Right now, Lily is the mission.

I reach her. She's covered in blood and mud, and finally there's a moon. Two, in fact. One shines down on us with a maternal glow. The other shines down on the bear. It grows suddenly, seven feet, eight feet, nine feet tall, expanding and spreading until it blocks out its own moon.

"He wants us, Duff, he wants both of us, he wants all of us. He won't stop until he has everything."

The bear says nothing. It just watches us. It knows.

It knows that it will win.

I shoot up out of my bed in a cold sweat, heart crashing against my ribs. The small rug next to my bed catches the soles of my feet. I don't slip, but I come damn close, reaching for my gun without thinking. My hand grasps cold metal, finger on the trigger, the weapon pointed at my window before I realize it was all a dream.

"What the hell?" I think to myself, standing there in my underwear, wind from the partly open window of my fourth-floor apartment making the sheer curtain flap inward. I must have heard it in my sleep. Translated it all into that crazy dream.

It's not the first time.

And definitely won't be the last.

This is one of the rare nights I get to stay home, if you call this place *home.* It's full of leftover furniture that someone at some agency picked up and threw together. Drew's agency covers the rent and utilities. When you work in the field like I do, you can't get attached to objects.

Not objects, not locations.

And certainly not *people.*

Lily.

She's obviously gotten inside me.

I start pacing, because that's what you do when you wake up in a cold sweat with a dream that won't disappear. The body stores memories. It's simple science. And when you're struggling with a fight between the emotional or psychological side of you and the body side of you, there's really only one good approach to finding your center again.

Beat the hell out of your body.

And where do you go to beat the hell out of your body?

To a gym.

As I set my weapon down on my bedside table, I look at the clock. 4:41 a.m. Screw the gym. I'll just run.

I'm supposed to be at Lily's at 6:30 to take her to another physical therapy appointment. Grabbing an old pair of shorts that I left on the floor the other day, I throw them on and slip my feet into socks and shoes for running. A ratty old t-shirt and I'm ready, keys in hand before I can even think about grabbing a bottle of water or taking a piss. I walk into the living room and head straight for the door.

The run is all I need right now.

Or at least that's the fiction I tell myself.

Just as my hand's on the doorknob, I realize I'm not alone in my living room.

And I don't have my gun.

CHAPTER 9

"*D*uff?"

I turn and look behind me, primal instincts standing down instantly. Lily's asleep on the couch where she insisted on staying last night. Or at least, she *was* asleep.

The nightmare threw me off. I should have remembered, but I didn't.

What the hell is wrong with me?

I reach up and run my shaking hand through short hair that feels messy. Chaotic. Out of control.

At least I didn't put myself in any jeopardy. More important, I didn't put *her* in any danger. It would have been easy to come out here with a gun drawn. I shoot to kill.

Tragic mistakes don't just happen to untrained civilians. It's easy to screw up when the adrenaline and the cortisol have taken over.

As I turn slowly and look at her, hair spread out against the pillow, body under a blanket that normally doesn't cover anyone but me, I take a deep breath, square my shoulders, unlock my knees and say, "Hey."

"Hey. Where are you going?"

"For a run."

"Oh." We stare at each other. I don't know what to say. In my dream, I couldn't find her. In my dream, I couldn't save her. Yet here she is on my couch, staring at me.

And I'm staring back.

"Do you always go running at–" her words cut off as she shoves a hand through her messy hair, pushing it off her brow. "What time is it, anyway?"

"About 4:45."

"Geez. Early bird gets the worm?"

"More like, early bird had a nightmare and couldn't go back to sleep."

I don't know why I say that. I don't know why I reveal something personal to her. Maybe it's the intimacy of having her here on my couch, seeing her clothes piled neatly on the chair at her feet, knowing that she's under that blanket of mine partly clothed, sleep still dusting her features.

Or maybe I'm just going soft.

Although one part of my body isn't.

"I don't want to go running," she whines as she grabs a pillow and shoves it over her head. Her muffled words make me laugh.

"Stay here. *I'm* just going for a run. You're fine."

"Aren't you supposed to guard me?"

"There's a whole team outside in the car. They've got you, too."

"You mean you're not it?"

"No. I'm not it."

"Why not?"

"I'm not it. Romeo's not it. None of us are it, Lily. Your case goes all the way up to the *president*."

"I know that."

"I know you know that. I'm trying to give you the background, the details that you keep asking about, so shut up for a minute and let me talk."

"Don't tell me to shut up."

"Do you want information or do you want to be right?" I ask her. She purses her lips, biting the lower one in a way that reminds me of our kiss.

I know what those lips taste like. Great.

Now I'm getting to the point where I can't run because these shorts are too tight.

"Go on," she says, propping her head up on one hand, her elbow against the pillow. "What is such a secret about the fact that you're not the only person watching me right now?"

"That's it. That's all you need to know. There's another team outside. They can keep an eye on you. I just need to go for a run." My heart is hammering in my chest. I can't admit to her that a part of me forgot for a few seconds that she was even *here*.

"How long are you going to be gone?"

"Three miles."

"That's a distance, Duff, not a time."

"I don't know. Three miles. However long it takes me to run three miles." If she keeps looking at me like that, it's going to take me an hour to run with this broomstick between my legs.

"Tell me more about all this behind-the-scenes stuff."

I groan. "Let me go for my run. When I come back, I'll tell you everything I'm allowed to."

"Will you bring me back a coffee?" she asks.

"Do I look like your errand boy?"

"Well, yes." She perks up. "You *are* my errand boy. You're protecting me. You help me. You're invested in my well-being. If I have to get up at 4:45 in the morning, my well-being includes coffee. Cinnamon latte. Almond milk."

"I know how you like your coffee, Lily."

"Then this is even easier." She's teasing me. She's killing me.

"I'm not going to get you any coffee, Lily, but," I hold up one finger to quell her protests, "I'll come back. I'm going to go for my run. When I get back here, be showered. Then I'll take a shower. And then we'll take you to your physical therapy appointment."

"I don't hear any coffee in there."

"I'll take you to my kind of coffee shop."

"I don't have the best track record with coffee shops these days, Duff."

"Trust me. This one isn't going to involve any gang-related shootings or anyone trying to finish the job they didn't do properly two years ago." The minute the word *properly* comes out of my mouth, I realize it's a mistake.

Her face confirms it.

"Lily, I didn't mean it that way."

"I know. I know," she says. She looks down, taking a deep breath. "I know you didn't mean it that way, but it's true."

"No one wants you dead."

"Oh, no, Duff. That's not true. Someone wants me very, very dead."

"We don't know that. They could have been aiming for Jane. Silas is going nuts about it and–"

"You really believe that," she interrupts.

"No," I say honestly. "I don't know. You–you take all of the clear-cut boundaries in the world, Lily, and you make them blur."

"I do?"

"Yeah. You do."

And with that, I grab the doorknob, open it, and leave.

Three miles takes me exactly nineteen minutes and forty-six seconds. I'm slow this morning. It's the first third of the run that requires some loosening up–if you know what I mean. By the time I'm back, she's sitting on the couch, reading some stupid magazine from five years ago that's from a magazine rack in this rat trap. Her hair's wet and she smells like my shampoo.

As I walk in the door, I grunt at her and go straight into the tiny bathroom, which also smells like my shampoo. Stripping out of my sweaty clothes, I climb in, trying damn hard not to think about the fact that she was just naked in the same space moments ago.

In the army, I learned to take a sixty-second shower. This one I manage in forty-nine. That's the advantage of short hair. I run a hand along the scruff on my jaw. I should shave. I know I should. Professional guidelines dictate that I need to, but I don't care about professional guidelines right now.

Nothing about my relationship with Lily is strictly professional anymore.

"I need coffee," she calls out as I throw on some clothes. My leg gets caught in one of the pants cuffs. I stumble and almost fall to the floor. I catch my hip on the bed, feet landing on the area rug.

It slides.

Once again, an object that is meant to protect turns into a vehicle for disaster. One hell of an allegory for life.

I come out of the bedroom nook to find her standing there, an expectant look on her face.

"Where to?" she asks.

"Physical therapy," I tell her. "Remember? 6:30."

"No. No. Before that, I need coffee. I know you're a coffee snob."

"I'm not a coffee *snob*," I protest. "I just like the really good stuff."

"Then show me the really good stuff, Duff," she says, her joints loose.

The joke's making me hard again. I turn away. I reach into my cupboard and pull out a small manual espresso maker, a device close to a one-shot French press. Filling the tea kettle, I turn on the burner and get things started.

"What's this?" she asks. "Aren't we supposed to go out for coffee?"

"Best coffee in town is right here, Lily."

"You're kidding. You're going to *make* coffee? What is that?" she asks, stumbling over her words as she watches me set up the espresso maker.

"This is how you make *real* coffee." I set the cone up over the coffee mug. Add the tiny circular filter. Screw it into place. Sprinkle exactly two level tablespoons of coffee grounds inside and then wait for the water to do its job.

"You make coffee like this every day? One cup at a time?"

"Only way to do it."

"It's so much effort."

"All the good things in life are."

We're bantering, laughing side by side. Having her in my personal space is disconcerting, but then again, this isn't really *my* space.

This is just a space that I occupy in the line of duty.

Is Lily someone I can occupy in the line of duty?

The kettle whistles. We both jump, taken by surprise at the known intrusion. I reach for the kettle handle and pour the water into the cylinder to make the coffee. She watches as I grab the paddle, swishing the hot water and grounds around, then slowly push the plunger down to produce the cup of espresso.

"This is like a French press," she observes. I shrug.

"Something like that."

The details don't matter. What matters is that I'm doing this with *her*. She asked me to invite her into my world and I did. There's no better way to do it than to show her what I like.

I hand her the cup of coffee. She wrinkles her nose.

"Got any almond milk?" she asks.

"No."

"Got any milk of any kind?"

"Yes. Cow's milk."

"I'm lactose intolerant."

"Sorry."

"Got any cinnamon?"

"Yes."

"I'm one for three."

For some reason, that makes me laugh as I reach into the cabinet and pull out the cinnamon.

She sprinkles it liberally on top.

"Go ahead," I tell her. "Trust me."

One wry eyebrow raises at my words. She takes a tentative sip. Her eyes light up.

"This is good."

"Told you. All that other stuff you've been drinking is crap."

She takes another sip. As her mouth wraps around the edge of the cup, I'm reminded of the fact that those lips once touched mine. "This is really good, Duff."

I take a partial bow.

"How does this thing work again?"

I slowly disassemble it, naming each part, pulling the dirty filter out and rinsing the contraption until I reassemble it, put a new filter in, add fresh grounds and reheat the water.

"It's a simple set of steps. Each methodical. Each important. You can't mix them up or get them out of order. They have to happen as intended."

Lily watches my hands moving through the steps as if following a rigid set of guidelines. She's smiling, sipping her coffee, chatting animatedly, and I ponder the fact that emotions don't have that kind of order.

I make my own cup of espresso and we go into the living room.

There's nowhere to sit other than the couch, so I take a spot next to her. She leans forward, casual and relaxed, elbows on the ends of her knees, the cup held up to her mouth. Steam rises off both of our drinks. The coffee is rich, with a cherry-and-caramel edge to it and smokehouse flavors that linger on my tongue.

This is exactly how I drink my coffee every morning, with the exception of Lily's presence. A guy could get used to this.

Tension in her shoulders drains out slowly as the coffee sinks in.

She looks at me, dark circles under her eyes, and asks, "I really have to do PT?"

"That's your choice," I say, taking another sip to shut up.

"I know I should go," she groans, "And I like Rhonda. Clem will probably be there. He's a creepy old guy, but he's harmless. It's just that going to PT is a reminder. It's a reminder of being shot. It's a reminder of being disabled. It's a reminder of all the ways that life is so much harder than it was supposed to be. I wasn't born like this, Duff. I was *made* like this. I had a dream last night," she says.

I jolt. "Yeah? What happened?"

"I was in a desert," she starts.

The hair on the back of my neck tingles.

"I was wandering completely alone, wearing this long, thin white robe. It flapped in the wind, like hands clapping. I walked slowly, until suddenly I wasn't walking on the sand. I was in the air, only I could walk. I could move. It was freeing. I opened up my arms and I stretched them out like that couple in *Titanic*. Like a bird flying with big wings. Only I wasn't flying. I was just walking. I heard you call my name. I turned and looked and there was this tent in the middle of the sand. Only that was *it*. There was nothing else. Not a single other person. No cars. No buildings. Nothing."

I don't know how to breathe.

Her eyes narrow as she looks over my shoulder, caught up in the memory. "You were in this tent. I could look and see the outside of the tent bulging like something inside was trying to get out. Except there was no door."

"You dreamt that? You dreamt about a tent?"

"Yeah. Did you dream about a tent last night, Duff?"

"No," I lie. "I don't dream."

"At all?"

"No. Not since I got back from Afghanistan."

"That's weird. My neurologist says that people who don't dream are rare. Maybe you dream and you just forget what the dream is about."

I stand. "It's time to go to PT."

"We have a few minutes, don't we? It's not far."

"Traffic."

She pulls her head back, offended by my abrupt words. "I don't care."

Chugging down the rest of my coffee, I reach for her empty cup, walk them into the kitchen, turn around, and walk straight out the front door, assuming she's behind me.

How the hell could Lily have had a dream just like mine? At what point did we become *that* connected? We get to the bottom of the second landing and I feel her hand on my shoulder.

"Duff," she says. I turn around. She's standing two steps above me. We're face to face. "Duff, that dream, there's a part of it I didn't tell you."

"What's that?"

"There was no door on that tent, but when I walked closer to the side of it, there was this bulging part. I realized it was a face."

"A face?"

"It was *your* face."

You ever kiss someone before you realize you're doing it? And you ever have them kiss you right back, twice as hard?

Her hands slide around my waist, slipping up under my jacket. Her fingers brush against my gun belt and I move, angling just enough to get it out of range. My hip twists just so, her pelvis connecting with mine. The kiss deepens. Just then both of our phones buzz.

She makes a guilty sound and pulls away, sticking her hand in her front pocket. She looks at the glass screen. "Reminder," she reads. "It's just a reminder of my appointment."

I look at mine. "Same."

"I think it's a reminder of a lot more," I say, pulling away, questioning every part of me in the blink of an eye.

"You said earlier that you wanted to talk about that kiss."

"I said that yesterday, Lily." *And now there's another.*

"Well," she says, leaning into my space, tilting forward until I have no choice but to hold her, "maybe we can talk about it now."

"What's there to talk about?"

"I think there's a lot to talk about, Duff. How about the fact that half the people involved in my security think that you're the one who tried to kill me and half think Romeo is the one who tried to kill me?"

"It doesn't matter what anybody else thinks, Lily. What matters is what *you* think. Who do you think tried to kill you?"

Long breaths fill the space between us. We smell like coffee. Like hope. Like two damaged people realizing that you can find something more than pain when you search long enough.

"What if I told you," she says, so serious, brow down, shoulders rigid, "that I don't have any new memories. Would you believe me?"

"I'd want to."

"That's not the same thing, Duff."

"I know it's not. Is it true though, Lily? I think you know

exactly who did it. I think you know his name. I think you know what he looks like. I think you're hiding him for a reason."

"Does that mean you think you know who it is?"

"Yes," I tell her.

"Then go ahead, Duff. Who do *you* think shot me?"

CHAPTER 10

I have to give her an out.

People need outs.

They need safe strategies for saving face. You don't get what you want by directly confronting someone who has something to hide. You have to make them *want* to share it.

For some people, that's all about ego. They want to prove they're smarter than you. That they're more powerful than you. They want to tell the thing that you are trying to unearth because they think it makes them look better. That it gives them more authority.

Other people just want to confess and get it over with.

And then there are the people who are hiding something for reasons that even they don't fully understand. They think it's for one reason, but it's really another. Those people are the hardest nuts to crack because the reason they're hiding something is often damn good.

"I'm going to give you a scenario, Lily. You tell me whether this hypothetical situation might be plausible."

"I'm not playing this game, Duff."

"You don't have a choice, Lily. You've been playing it all along."

Fear flashes through her eyes.

"Fine."

"'There is no greater agony than bearing an untold story inside you,'" I whisper. "Maya Angelou said that."

"You're quoting literature to me? Now? *Really*, Duff?"

I shrug. I expect to get an eye roll in return.

I don't.

So I press on.

"Hypothetically, there's a young woman working in a flower–in a greeting card shop. And she's working at the counter with her back turned to the front door. She hears the door open. She looks up, but she doesn't turn around. And then *bam!* Shot in the back of the head. What could she have looked at from her vantage point to have allowed her to see her killer?"

She sighs heavily. "Her 'killer' didn't kill her, so he's not really her killer. He's just a crazed asshole who decided to shoot her, Duff."

"Fine. The crazed asshole who *tried* to kill her."

She smirks. "Well, *hypothetically*," she says, "she could have caught a whiff of his cologne. Or she could have seen his image in a piece of glass, like a picture frame, or a window, or—"

I cut her off. "A mirror?" Her lips are parted, the white edges of her teeth showing.

She licks her lower lip and says, "Yeah, sure. A mirror."

"Okay."

"Okay..." Lily says. She's still standing on that stair. We're still eye to eye. I peer at her.

"And let's say that greeting card woman nearly dies, over and over, throughout the course of the first week after the shooting. But she's a fighter. She's strong. She comes back. She's unconscious. No one can talk to her. In fact, the doctors give up on her. But her parents don't. Neither does her bodyguard."

There's a stillness to her that makes me ache.

"And then one day, fourteen months after the shooting, on the night that Harwell Bosworth wins the presidency of the United States, she wakes up. Coincidence?"

It's clear she didn't anticipate *that* turn in the conversation.

"What do you mean, coincidence? It's not like I *planned* to be

63

unconscious for fourteen months and spontaneously wake up on the night he won. What are you implying?"

"I'm not implying anything, Lily. I'm being hypothetical, remember? Nobody's talking about *you*."

"Of course we're talking about me, you idiot."

She gets a pass on the insult.

"This greeting card woman comes out of her coma and her personality's different. She's still the same person. No question there. No doppelgängers, no body swapping going on here. But she's harder, tighter, more closed off, colder."

"I'm not cold."

I shrug. "She's that way–*hypothetically*–because she's keeping a secret. She knows the identity of her killer. She has evidence that she hasn't revealed to anyone else. What would it take for people who care about her to get the truth out of her?"

As I say the words, "care about her," I reach up and stroke her cheekbone, pulling a piece of hair away and sliding it behind her ear. The cinnamon from her morning coffee tickles my nose.

She curls her face into my hand.

"She would, well... she would need to know that the killer can't ever hurt her or her mom, or dad, or siblings." The words come out haltingly as she trembles. "She would need to know that the killer isn't being helped by other people in her life."

I'm close. I'm so close.

"What could someone say to this woman to convince her of all that?"

She gives a sad smile. The edges of her lower lip start to tremble. The skin underneath her eyes goes tight. Her gaze catches mine. We're inches apart and I could kiss her again, but I know that would be a mistake.

"You really think there's a way out for her?" she asks.

"I do."

"How?"

"How can I help you to be safe and protect your family from the guy who tried to kill you?"

"No," she says, hand up in a gesture that says I need to stop talking. "That's not the question. How can you stand there in

64

front of me after kissing me like that and tell me everything will be okay when you *know* there's no way out?"

"If I thought there was no way out, Lily, I wouldn't be here."

"And if I thought there *was* a way out, Duff, I wouldn't be here, either."

"What does that mean?"

"It means, *hypothetically*," she says slowly, "that you're asking me to give you information I don't have."

The tipping point happened.

I lost.

She's gone over the edge. Or maybe *I'm* the one who's gone over the edge. There's no backtracking here. But I'm planting seeds, and seeds, when exposed to sunlight, eventually have to grow.

"Lily, you don't have to tell me anything."

"I know."

"But if you did, if you were going to give me one shred of information, I would ask this: Is the person who tried to kill you standing in this stairwell with you?"

I just handed her my heart. Pulled it straight out of my chest and held it up, waiting for her to take it.

She kisses me instead, a quick press of the lips, like signing a contract.

Lips still on mine, she murmurs, "No."

CHAPTER 11

"These muscles aren't gonna fix themselves," Lily says to me, pushing past me on the stairs, the change jarring. "Let's go to physical therapy. Rhonda's waiting, and besides, they have crap coffee there."

I play her game. I groan and hold the door open for her.

Early morning sunshine, not quite blinding, greets us as we head out into the short corridor before turning into the parking garage.

"Why would you drink that crap at PT?"

She shrugs. "It's a caffeine delivery system." We're both trying to find our way out of what just happened. I get that. It's fine. What's more important than the actual result of our conversation is that she starts to trust me even more.

The kiss was a fringe benefit.

It's a short drive to the physical therapy unit where Lily gets her treatment. I pull into the parking lot. The same space I always take is available.

"Why do you park here?" she asks.

"Because in the beginning you were in a wheelchair, and then the walker. It was easier to get you into the building through the handicapped section."

"But you had a handicapped sticker back then."

66

"I did, and then when we didn't, I just parked in the same spot."

She twists in her seat and faces me as if she's going to reach to touch me, but she doesn't.

"Don't do that anymore," she says, her voice dismissive, as if I've offended her. "Don't park here. Park as far away as possible in the lot, and make me work for it."

"Yes, ma'am."

We get out and walk into the building. She peels off to go to the women's locker room. I stand around and try to pretend I'm useful. You don't work out after a three-mile run, so I get to be decoration.

As expected, old Clem is there. He waves to me. I nod back.

Lily comes out and asks, "Do you remember the name of that sports cream we learned about, the one that's so good for dealing with sore muscles?" She bends down, massaging her right calf, looking up at me in a way that is achingly vulnerable.

"No." It takes everything in me not to kiss her.

"It's on the tip of my tongue," she says as she straightens.

"I got something that would love the tip of your tongue, sweets!" Clem shouts.

"That's enough," I growl.

"Hey, man, at my age, all I got is words."

"You're gonna lose teeth if you keep that shit up, Clem," I add.

Lily gives me a wry grin. My tone is light but I can tell it bothers her to have Clem making jokes like that. Just because he isn't directly threatening doesn't mean he isn't gross.

And way out of line.

"Hey, you," says Rhonda, coming from around a rack of weights. "What are you doing here?" she says to me. "I thought you were being reassigned."

I halt. "Reassigned?"

"Yeah. That's what Romeo said."

"Romeo was here?" Lily's question echoes mine.

"Yeah. He came in a couple of days ago. Said Duff would be reassigned. Checked out the security, and said something about a shooting. You okay?" she asks Lily.

"I'm fine. Long story. It turns out there's a reason I've got a security detail," she says looking at me with a sheepish grin.

"Wait. You mean someone tried to kill you *again?*" Rhonda clarifies.

"Yeah."

"And you're this calm?"

"I'm either calm or shell shocked, I'm not sure which one."

"She's calm," I tell them both. "A little too calm."

"What does that mean?" Lily protests.

"It means for someone who isn't in the field, you've got a really good hold on your emotions."

"And that's bad?"

"It's just–"

"Weird," Rhonda interrupts. "Emotions get stored in the body, Lily," she elaborates. "You need to get this stuff out."

"I need to get *what* out?"

"You need to get your shock, horror, gratitude, your..." Rhonda thinks for a minute. "All of it. I can sit here with you and give you rotational movements and specific exercises that can help you to take care of the body's trauma from the shooting two years ago, but none of that will make much difference if you don't process the emotions."

"I *am* processing the emotions. I work with psychiatrists and psychologists. You guys know that."

"You *worked* with a psychiatrist," Rhonda says pointedly, "but you rejected that doctor on the grounds that you don't need psychotropic drugs anymore."

"I don't."

"But you need a therapist."

"I don't," Lily digs in. "Anymore."

Rhonda's palms go up in a gesture of placating. "Look, Lily, I'm not here to argue with you. I'm sorry. I'm just here to work with you. But if people are still shooting at you, I think that alone is enough to qualify as trauma, whether you're hit or not."

Lily's face hardens. "Just tell me how you're going to torture me today."

Rhonda grins. "There's always the really bad coffee."

That gets a smile out of Lily. "I started my day with really good coffee, actually. Duff gave me some of his."

Rhonda gives me some attention. "You know a good place?"

"I know a good machine."

"What does that mean?"

Lily chuckles. "You don't want to know."

"What? Do you use old underwear as a filter for making your coffee, Duff?"

Lily grabs a kettle bell, smirking, as my phone buzzes. Rhonda laughs and joins her, starting warmup exercises.

It's a text from Romeo. *What the hell was yesterday about?* he texts.

Only getting back to me now? I reply.

The president has questions about you, he texts back.

Oh, I'm sure he does, I reply quickly. *Does he want a meeting with me? I hear he's hiring.*

You wish, Romeo sends back. *You need to keep that girl on a leash.*

What girl? I text back.

You know exactly who I'm talking about is his reply.

"Duff?"

I look up from the text stream to see Jane Borokov standing there. "Jane. What are you doing here?"

"I came to talk to you."

I shove the phone in my pocket. Suddenly Romeo isn't a priority. Having Jane appear at the physical therapy center for Lily is odd, to say the least.

"Come over here," I tell her, pulling her into a little alcove off the main exercise-equipment area. "What's going on?"

"I wanted to talk to you about what happened in that meeting."

"Fertile ground, huh?"

"No kidding," she says with a long sigh. "But what I really want to talk about is Romeo."

"What about him?" The guy is everywhere.

"Keep him away from Lily."

That's blunt. And revealing.

"Why?"

"Can't you tell?"

"You mean, the way she went off on him yesterday? Talked about how he was treating her family?"

"That. And more."

She's nervous, and that's not Jane's normal demeanor. Ever since she inherited an enormous amount of money from her art professor, Alice Mogrett, and since she fell out of the media spotlight after Monica Bosworth tried to kill Harry and took the focus off Jane, she's been more confident, more herself. The person in front of me is jumpy and timid.

And she's talking about Romeo.

I don't think the two are unrelated.

"Something happened with Romeo that I think you should know about," she says softly. "I was telling Lily this story when the gunman opened fire in the coffee shop."

"Really?"

"I know. The timing's bizarre. That's why Lily thinks someone's bugging her. She can't believe that it's unconnected."

"What were you talking about?"

"I was telling her about the night in the sex club."

I bristle. I can't help it. "Are you sure we should be having this conversation?"

"It's not *that* kind of story, Duff. I'm talking about when I was kidnapped and almost assaulted by Nolan Corning."

"What about it?"

"Romeo was there."

"Yeah, I know. He helped."

She blinks over and over, as if in a trance, and then looks at me.

"He *helped*? That's a funny way of saying it, Duff. Who do you think he helped?"

"What do you mean?"

"Who do you think he was helping? Was he helping me, or was he helping Corning?"

"You're alive. You're standing here in front of me asking me questions two years later. I have to assume that he was helping you. If he wanted you dead, you'd be dead."

"When you say 'he,' who do you mean?" she asks softly. "Nolan Corning or Romeo?"

"Who do *you* mean, Jane?"

"You're evading my questions, Duff."

"No, ma'am, I'm not evading them. I'm simply making sure I understand where this conversation is going."

"This conversation is about making sure you know about him."

"Him?"

"Romeo. I was hiding in the room that night. Silas had left me in there and locked me in. Someone turned the key and on instinct I tried to hide. There was a curtain with an opening behind it. Kind of a secret passageway, only I didn't know it at the time. I hid behind the curtain and waited. And in came Nolan Corning. He had a key. I didn't know where he got the key. Corning walked into the room and just before he reached me, Romeo appeared right behind me."

I interrupt her. "I've read the reports."

"What I'm about to tell you isn't in any reports, Duff."

I roll my shoulders and lean in. "Go ahead."

Out of the corner of my eye, I see Lily racking weights, Rhonda talking to her, pointing. The two are engaged in the standard back and forth of physical therapy. I've seen it a hundred times in recent months.

But in these moments, as they unfold with Jane's story coming out, it seems so domestic, so normal in its simplicity.

Whatever Jane's about to say isn't normal.

"It was the way he grabbed me, Duff. He grabbed me from behind and covered my mouth. His other hand—well, it's just... Look," she says staring up at the ceiling, avoiding eye contact, "I know the difference between a security grab for the sake of keeping me safe and hands like *that*. And it was his words. He said things that you could take in multiple ways."

She sighs.

"Like what? This is the first I've heard about what he said to you."

"I know. I didn't even say anything to Silas for a long time, because it's–what he said, his words were innocuous. It's *how* he said it that was so horrible."

"Go ahead. I won't judge."

"I can't remember it word for word, but it went something like this: *I don't want what happened to Lily to happen to you.*"

My eyebrows shoot to the moon.

"He said that? What else?"

"And then he said: *I'm here, sweetheart. I'm here to do my job. Don't move. It will all be over soon.*"

"Holy shit. No one told me this."

She gives me the same look I've given people a thousand times.

"I've been driving myself nuts thinking about those words, because I still have no idea which side he was on." Scared eyes meet mine. "Was he protecting me?"

After a short pause, she asks:

"Or something else?"

CHAPTER 12

"What are you implying, Jane?"

"I'm the one Lily's shooter was trying to kill. I'm still alive two years later, and it's not just because of Silas. Something is going on beneath the surface here that no one understands."

"Right."

"Let me be clear," she says, leaning forward, putting her hand on my elbow. "I don't think you did it. I know that there *are* people who think you did it, but I'm not one of them. I also think, after that meeting with the president–"

She cuts her words off.

I notice she doesn't call him her father.

Continuing, she adds, "I think there's something really suspicious going on with Romeo." Concern floods her features. "And I think we need to talk about getting Lily out of here."

"Out of here? The gym?"

"No. Out of town. I've already talked to Silas and Drew about this. I want Lily to come to my place."

"The ranch? In Texas?"

"Yes." Her brow furrows as she looks around, furtive and worried. "I'm still in the process of going through Alice's old papers."

As she speaks, I have to keep myself completely self-contained. Can't show any emotion.

"There's a lot of work to do on the ranch, and it's quiet. A haven. Lily needs a haven right now. She needs a place where she can just rest."

"If anyone knows about that, it's you."

"No kidding." She relaxes a little. That helps.

"Why should Lily come to the ranch with you?" I ask her. "She has a place to live. She has parents, a sister, a brother, and a whole host of medical professionals here who are helping her to recover."

Jane gives me a twisted smile. "You know exactly why."

"I do?"

"Lily may need to recover, but what she needs more is a break. Right now, her entire identity is wrapped up in being Trauma Girl. She's got paparazzi following her for a photo of the miracle woman who recovered from a shooting to the back of the head. There are tabloids talking about her alongside me, and conflating the two of us for click bait. She's got an actual killer on her trail, trying to cover up his tracks and still threatening her. I think a ranch in Texas that's used to high levels of security and that is about as locked down as you can get is the safest place on Earth for her. Plus, Duff," she says with a long sigh, "I feel awful."

I stare at her. Guilt unites Jane and me.

"If she and I didn't look alike, if there hadn't been this mistaken identity, or if I'd been the one at that counter when the guy came in to kill me, n-none of this would've happened to Lily." She stammers. The sudden shift to an emotional plea throws me off guard.

"Got it," I say, buttoning up my emotions. "You're making good points."

"Whether I'm making good points or not doesn't matter," she says quickly. "Because it's a done deal."

"What do you mean it's a done deal?"

"We're going. Lily is coming with me right after this."

"Wait. Have you cleared this with her?"

"No."

"Have you cleared this with her mother and father?"

"No."

"Then why are you saying it's definitely happening?"

"Because I'm about to go over to her and convince her to come."

"You think you're going to change Lily's mind?"

"I don't think I have to change Lily's mind. I think I just have to lay it out in a way that makes her see reason."

I make a dismissive noise before I can stop myself. "She's not seeing a lot of reason these days."

"Maybe not, but she's seeing an awful lot of clarity."

I have to agree with that.

"Fine," I tell her, "I'll get ready. We have to do a background check on some of the security." I stop myself. "Wait, no, we won't. It's already been done by Gentian and Foster."

"Right. It's perfect," she says. "Lily gets a break, I get to spend some time with her, and we're both sequestered in a place that someone would have to be insane to try to breach."

This time, my laughter is bitter. "Remember the shootings at The Grove? Do you remember the shooting in your father's townhouse in DC? If you think there's any place, anywhere, that's unbreachable, Jane, you're naïve."

"No, Duff," she says softly, "not naïve. Just hopeful and trusting." She moves her hand off my arm. "The safest place on Earth is one with you, Silas, and Drew in charge, and that's my ranch in Texas."

She turns and walks away, leaving me with those final words: *my ranch in Texas.*

It's impossible to think of it that way, as Jane's ranch. For so many years, it was Alice Mogrett's.

I can't let myself think about Alice right now, any more than I can let myself think about the countless people who have died over the last two years in this mess that Lily finds herself entangled in.

My phone buzzes at the same time that I hear Lily let out a

grunt of effort. She drops a forty-five pound weight. Rhonda fist bumps her. Lily doesn't smile back.

We've kissed twice now with no follow up to figure out what the hell it means. But it means something, right? It has to. Actions without meaning are performed by a robot. I might be a robot when it comes to my job, but not when it comes to Lily.

I look at my phone. It's a text from Gentian. *Get Lily on a plane to Jane's ranch. Now. And bring a bag.*

I know what *bring a bag* means. Means I'm on detail. Back when I worked at Alice Mogrett's ranch full time, I didn't need a bag. I had a set of work clothes there and a small room where all of the security detail rotated spending the night. Once Jane took over, Foster put an end to my work there and assigned me to Lily.

Roger, I write back.

Thought you were Duff, he replies.

Old joke. Still not funny.

I tally up what I've learned this morning. Jane trusts me. Lily mostly does. Gentian must, or he wouldn't have me on detail at his girlfriend's ranch. Foster, too.

Romeo doesn't. And the president of the United States *definitely* doesn't.

Lily's parents are on the fence, and Romeo is working on them, against me. The percentages aren't that great when it comes to figuring out where I am in the balance here. Are the people who *do* trust me enough to give me leverage? To give me access? To make Lily truly believe in me?

Or are we all being manipulated by a mastermind, five levels deeper than we ever imagined?

Out of the corner of my eye, I see Jane talking to Lily, Lily's look of surprise morphing into something close to anger. Her eyes narrow. Her mouth opens. The words come out rapid fire, like bullets. Jane nods, intently listening. Even from afar, it's clear she's attuned to Lily's signals and her words.

Jane speaks again.

Lily's hands go to her hips, a stance that makes me study her even more carefully. She's intuitively finding her own power.

Most people shrink from it. That's understandable. We're trained by society to be that way, or there would be too many leaders and not enough followers. It doesn't work in a hierarchical structure to have too many leaders.

We have to find ways to make people relinquish their own authority.

Until the shooting, Lily fit into that social structure. She was happy, a bright light in an industry designed to give people joy–through something that eventually just withers and dies.

An interesting paradox.

So is the Lily she was before the shooting and the Lily she is now, as well as the Lily she is becoming. You don't change like that unless there's an underlying structure in place, deep inside the self, that's been there all along.

Lily's strength is so central to her core that I don't think even she realizes how deep it goes.

We have primal selves that get activated in times of great stress or great change. A psy-ops trainer back in the army taught me this. People don't really change if they're exposed to trauma.

They just become more of who that primal self is.

Or they put their mind to it and do the work.

And for Lily, it's both.

CHAPTER 13

*G*uys like me aren't supposed to exist.

But we do.

And we serve a purpose.

Some of us don't even have birth certificates. I'm not one of them. I am a real person, with a family and a core identity. Some of us don't even have that.

They're considered the lucky ones.

I'm not so sure I agree.

When you have no past, no foundation, no roots, it's really hard to stay centered. People without an anchor are dangerous.

People in jobs like mine need to be internally driven. We respond to external stimulation. That's the whole point.

We *respond*.

We don't *react*.

We don't let ourselves get triggered by the ebb and flow of life around us. We are steady. We are invisible. But we are always watching.

You can't do that when you don't exist.

There's a yin and yang to being in this job. The internal and the external. If you don't have any roots, or an identity of your own, then the external takes hold. If everything you do is driven by forces outside yourself, then the wrong external force can turn you evil.

That may be an extreme, but I see it in a lot of the guys who don't know who they are. Who have no record of a day when they emerged into the world vulnerable, innocent, connected.

How do people function without a birth certificate? Sure, it's just a piece of paper. Nothing more, nothing less. Simply an official document that says, "You are."

It's easy to dismiss something like that as trivial. But documentation matters. Especially when it comes to your very existence. If no one knows you're there, what can you get away with? That's the whole point. That's why these people get recruited by the deep state.

Because when no one knows you are there, there are no limits to what you can do.

My phone buzzes. It's a text from Drew. It says, *ETD?*

I type back, *10 minutes*

His response is immediate and simple, *K.*

I look up. Lily is staring at me. I *definitely* exist when she's staring at me.

And there you have it.

That's the danger of being anchored. Of knowing who you are, even when no one around you can see you. Lily sees me now. Lily wants to see me.

And I want to be seen.

I have to hold those truths in my head at the same time. I have to hold two *selves* in my head at the same time—two versions of myself. The one who knows how to implement and execute a mission. And the one who is a human being.

We are not allowed to be human beings when we're working.

But we can't just be robots, either.

Guys like Romeo are as close as they come to being robots, though.

There's a sharpness about Romeo I don't like.

I don't mean intelligence. I'm talking about something else.

Most people have blurred lines. Their edges are indistinct. It makes them softer, more human.

He's the other way around.

"Mom, I'm not arguing with you," Lily tells Bee on the phone as we wait in the hangar for the go-ahead to board the plane to Texas. "I'm doing this."

Pause. I hear a very upset Bee on the other end just as my phone rings.

Two guesses who that is.

Tom, the screen says as I accept the call.

"Duff," he says before I can even give a greeting. "Promise me this is safe."

"I promise."

"Bee's losing it."

"I can hear. Lily's right here on the phone with her."

"Lily says the shooting at the coffee shop was the tip of the iceberg? And she's rambling about some meeting with the president, who happens to be here in California at his private home? The neurologists warned us that there could be long-term paranoia and hallucinations associated with the shooting and the brain injury—"

I cut him off. "Every word she's telling you is real, Tom. There is more to the shooting at the coffee shop. We believe Lily and Jane were directly targeted."

A low whistle is all I get in response.

"And she did meet with President Bosworth," I confirm. Gentian gave the clear on saying that to her parents.

"Why did he want to meet with our Lily?"

"I can't say."

"Were you there?"

"Yes."

"Then you damn well can."

"No, Tom—I mean I *can't say*."

"This cloak-and-dagger shit gets old fast."

No kidding.

"Tell me I can trust you," he pleads. "Tell me I'm not a stupid man who is putting his daughter in the hands of a liar."

"I promise you I'll keep her safe."

I can't promise him I'm not a liar, though.

"Bee's so upset."

"I'm sure she is."

"She doesn't trust you."

I stay silent.

"Romeo says you can't be trusted."

"I'd go with your gut on this one, Tom."

"Lily trusts you."

That makes me feel better than it should.

"And I believe my daughter."

"She's worth being believed."

At those words, Lily catches my eye and gives me a grateful smile.

Then she goes back to being angry with her mother.

"She's twenty-five. A mature young woman. We had her young and then we waited awhile before having Bowie and Gwennie. She's always been so sweet and friendly. The happiest child you've ever met. She was like helium, you know? You always felt so good when you spent time with Lily."

I know, Tom. I know.

"And to think that some nutcase targeted *her*, out of all the people in the world. That he thought she was Jane Borokov was bad enough—but now he's back and really trying to kill her? Why?"

"We don't know."

"Is it because she's telling you guys something we don't know?"

"Like what?"

"Like—like new memories?"

"Why are you asking me this, Tom? Why not ask your daughter?"

"Because Bee's convinced she's lying to us. Lying to everyone. And so is Romeo."

"What does my co-worker have to do with this?" I ask, knowing the answer to my own question, but asking it anyway.

"He's—how close are you two?"

"We're colleagues."

"I mean—" He lets out an aggravated breath. "I don't know who I can trust."

"Can't blame you."

81

"You're no help, Duff."

"Sorry, man."

"What would you do in my position?" he asks, clearly hating himself for it. I get it. When you don't know who you can trust, you finally weaken with the person you have some kind of connection to, even if it's a bad connection. Tom and Bee blame me for Lily's shooting.

Maybe for both shootings, now.

But I'm familiar. That's another reason why we have long-term security details: being familiar is a tactical advantage.

"I can't tell you what to do, Tom." I know my words are meaningless, but I have to say them, and they have to be true. I don't know what I would do in his position, but I do know that I have to keep his trust.

"I'm damned if I do and I'm damned if I don't, aren't I?" he says with a cynical hiss that makes me square my shoulders.

I start to pace. Out of the corner of my eye, I see Lily engaged in her argument with Bee, her hands animated and gesturing, even though her mother's on the other side of a phone. If I weren't talking to her father and needing every bit of brain power, I'd laugh.

It's amusing how our integrated bodies process data. Lily's conscious mind knows that her mother isn't there and can't see her, and yet we have mirror neurons. Those neurons make us more human. We instinctively act out what we see and what we imagine. Parts of our brain light up from that kind of imaginary connection, even when we're not physically doing an activity or physically in front of another person.

Lily can't help herself. She is deeply, intimately human. Her father can't help himself, either. Faced with the impossible task of deciding who is best positioned to help his daughter, and knowing that it's not him, he has to make a decision.

Fortunately for me, he chooses well.

"I don't understand what's going on with Romeo," he says. "The guy keeps calling Bee and convincing her that Lily is holding back. And Lily *is* holding back. We know it. We know our daughter, and our daughter trusts you, Duff. By some sort of transitive property, that means we need to trust you. So let me say this: Take her away. Take her away to Jane Borokov's ranch and keep her safe. Keep her safe until she gets to the point where she trusts someone in this mess enough to tell them whatever it is that's eating her from the inside out."

"You really think she's holding back, Tom?" I ask.

"I do, and I don't understand why she's continuing to hide something from everyone. Has she told you?" he asks, knowing damn well I wouldn't give any sort of real answer even if I knew.

"No," I say, telling the truth. "She hasn't."

"Then get her to. Use whatever magic skills they give you guys to pry it out of her."

"That's not how it works."

"I know," he says. "But try. She's a stubborn one. Takes after her mother."

As I watch Lily's face fill with anger at whatever her mother's saying to her on the phone, I smile.

"I've got to trust someone, Duff. Might as well be you," he says, and then ends the call, leaving me staring at my own glass screen as Lily chucks her phone against the wall–

–and it shatters.

CHAPTER 14

*S*ilverton, Texas is an unlikely place to have an impromptu safehouse.

But for now, it will do.

And as Jane said—it's about as secure and locked down as you can get.

The descent is uneventful, Lily wide awake as the tires squeal on the runway, the pilot experienced enough to make rubber and asphalt converge like we're landing on butter.

A line of black SUVs, five in all, are parked against the main building of this tiny airport. All of them, I suspect, are part of Drew Foster's company. Since Alice Mogrett died, I also suspect they get slightly less use.

Then again, Jane is her heir.

Maybe I'm wrong.

Alice Mogrett was the child of a U.S. vice president who later became a beloved and respected Supreme Court justice. A self-described wild child, she was the talk of the town in the 1950s and 1960s, known for forming and living in communes, anti-war protests, and for a deep appreciation of art.

That turned into a radical understatement.

She became a well-known artist in her lifetime, unlike most, and settled into a professorship at Yates University in her fifties, at a time when most people are looking to retire. Jane Borokov was her student, and later a subject of her paintings—all nudes—but the most important role Jane had in Alice's life was friend.

And then heir.

Inheriting eight figures from a controversial character was destabilizing for Jane, who was Public Enemy #1 when Alice died. Worse was having Alice die while Jane was here at the ranch, spending the night as a guest. I should know.

I was here, too.

I help Lily into one of the SUVs, driven by Ralph, a guy I barely know but have worked alongside for two years. Blond, Nordic, sharp cheekbones, all hard edges. He's one of those guys who don't exist. Not on paper, not on the internet, not anywhere. Paid in secret, never in a database, and completely, coolly designed to be the human equivalent of an airbag in a car:

You only know it's there when you need it to save your life.

Watching Lily as she sees the ranch from a great distance, the flatland unrolling in an endless plane, makes me smile. I remember the first time I was summoned to Alice Mogrett's place.

It was a lot longer ago than anyone here knows.

The unpaved road kicks up dust that some guy like Ralph will have to wash off once we're done delivering our clients. It's part of the job, and it never bothered me. You clean the black SUV. Keep it pristine. People want what they want and if the boss orders it—you do it.

Beats stewing in your own thoughts at the same time that you're supposed to be blank and vigilant.

The Mogrett ranch gives meaning to the word *sprawling*. The windows are covered in dust, but the colonial feel of the house makes you look twice. Lily presses her face against the car window, her nose bending slightly, enthralled.

The house has a white peak right in the middle, almost like a church in a small town. But make no mistake: this isn't a house of worship. It's a house owned by one of the most notorious women of the twenty-first century.

Black shutters border the windows. The symmetry of the original structure itself is somehow quaint and militaristic at the same time. The wings added to either side of the original house, though, make the ranch distinctive. On the right, there's a single-story wing that spreads out the way that land in Texas takes over. It's the footprint of the main house minus the other stories.

On the left side, there's a double-story wing with an enormous porch up on the second floor. A windowed solarium is below it. Alice liked to paint there until she created her studio. I remember vines creeping up, hugging exposed beams, before extensive remodeling changed that.

As if they're a security line, there's a row of large trees, full and weeping, standing like drunken soldiers daring a windstorm to take them out.

It's a home that says: This is a place of authority.

It's a home that says: This is a place of power.

It's a home that I've guarded for longer than I'm allowed to share.

Ralph pulls the SUV up to the front door. Lily steps out, grabbing sunglasses from Jane as she offers them.

"What's this for?"

"Trust me. You'll want them," Jane says.

When you look at the property, you realize it's *all* white. The trees break up the whiteness. The house itself is painted white, black shutters the only contrast. The trees provide contrast, too, but surrounding the buildings are white rock gardens. It's a study in dark and light, just like Alice Mogrett.

"This is where you live?" Lily whispers to Jane, who shrugs and smiles. She slides an arm around Lily's shoulders and turns her towards the front entrance.

"Come on in. I'll give you a tour."

"I don't have three hours for that," Lily says, deadpan.

Jane laughs, "How about we just go to the part of the house that I like the most?"

"Which part is that?"

"It's actually not even here in the house. It's Alice's old studio."

"Where's that?"

86

"It's on the right side of the house, under the pergola."

"Wait a minute." Lily halts as her foot hits the first step of the large entrance. "You have all this and you choose to live in a little guest house behind it?"

"Pretty much."

Silas gives Lily a smile. "I've been saying the same thing to her myself."

"I like what I like," Jane shrugs.

"No kidding."

The kiss he gives Jane on the temple changes the air around us. Lily tenses, but then relaxes more.

"Let's get you inside," I say, my hand going between her shoulder blades. The gentle nudge is more than enough to get her to move. This place is crawling with plenty of security, but after the shooting at the coffee shop, no place feels secure.

Having her stay at my apartment was an emergency measure. Having her here is smart strategy.

Jane takes us through the large foyer and straight through to the back of the house. We cut to the right through a small rock garden, and then there it is: Alice's old studio.

The word *studio* doesn't do it justice. It's a three-bedroom guest house with a full kitchen, three and a half baths, and an enormous living room designed for large-scale painting. Alice was an oil painter. As we step into the studio, the paint smell hits me, taking me back too far.

Way too far.

"This is where you live?" Lily's eyes jump between Silas and Jane, her implication clear: The "you" means both of them.

"Yes," Jane says, going over to the kitchen. She reaches into the refrigerator and pulls out a pitcher of lemonade with a sprig of mint floating on top. "Lemonade?" she asks Lily.

"Sure."

"Vodka?" she asks.

"What?"

"You want a vodka lemonade?"

Lily looks at the clock. "It's not even four here. And in California it's even earlier."

"Alice always drank vodka with her lemonade." Jane frowns. "Not always, but most of the time."

"Do you have to do everything that Alice did?" Lily asks. "Is it a requirement for inheriting all of this?"

Silas bites his lower lip and tries not to laugh.

"No, there are no requirements on the will. I inherited it all free and clear." Jane pours a shot of vodka into two of the four glasses, and then fills them all with lemonade. She knows not to add vodka to Silas's and mine. We'd both reject it. You have to stay sharp when you're on duty. Silas's passing on the vodka tells me everything I need to know about this trip.

We're on duty 24/7.

Lily accepts her glass with a surprisingly steady hand and sips gingerly. Her eyes light up.

"That's really good."

"There's lavender and mint in there," Jane tells her.

The domestic nature of the scene is jarring. On the surface, we're two men and two women having a glass of lemonade as we stay out of the Texas afternoon sun on a ranch that's as beautiful as it is functional. That's all you would see if you looked at the surface. Underneath, the layers teem and roil with controversy, with mortality, with scandal.

Then again, the same could be said for Alice Mogrett.

I take in the room. The furniture is exactly as it was two years ago, though Jane has different lamps, and framed photos of her and Silas's families dot the flat surfaces. Silas's seven-year-old niece, Kelly, grins a gap-toothed smile, wet hair plastering her face as she plays on a beach. An older picture of Jane and her mother, Anya, riding horses. A picture of Linda, Silas's mother, walking hand-in-hand with Kelly. A picture of Jane, Silas, and Kelly hiking on a mountaintop.

A happy family.

If you didn't know the pain and loss they've all endured in the last three years, you'd think they live perfect lives. Jane's mother died in jail, Kelly's mother–Silas's sister, Tricia–died of a heroin overdose. And of course Tricia was also Linda's daughter.

But the photos tell a different story. A new one. O₁ future that isn't suffocated by the past.

Maybe the phoenix really can rise from the ashes, reborn.

I blink, hard.

Lily's halfway through her drink before I hear her sigh. Jane leads us over to one of the sitting areas in the big, open space. She's left all of the artwork up, including a couple of nude paintings of Jane herself.

Doesn't take long for Lily to notice.

Her eyes go wide, lips parting. She can't help but stare. Her hand holds the thin iced-tea glass full of lemonade. She fixes on the large painting in front of her, her head tipped up to the sky like a child enjoying a sudden rainburst. She's too polite to ask, and Silas and Jane share an amused look.

"Like the art?" Jane asks in a voice that's half joking, half embarrassed.

"That's you!"

"Yes."

"Alice Mogrett painted *you*?"

"You knew that, didn't you?"

A head shake. More wide eyes. "I know who she is. I know she was your teacher and friend. But you never mentioned..." Lily points to the painting, "...that."

"Does it make you uncomfortable?" I ask her quietly.

"No. It's beautiful. The naked body is a joyful playground," Lily whispers to me.

And just like that, I can't breathe.

CHAPTER 15

"*H*ere," Silas says to Lily, handing her a thin, black phone. I watch, the rest of them oblivious to the internal torture I'm experiencing. That's fine.

That's how it all works.

My emotions don't matter. They never matter. In fact, they get in the way of my mission.

"We got you a replacement," he tells her. Smart man. He didn't have to give her the device right at this moment, but it breaks the tension.

Or, at least, *my* tension.

"Thanks. I shouldn't have thrown my other one. How much do I owe you?" she asks him, suddenly frowning as she lets money enter her list of things to worry about.

Silas smiles at her. "There's no bill for anything we do for you, Lily. You know that."

She looks at Jane, suddenly helpless. "I don't have a blueprint for any of this."

"Blueprint?"

"You pay for everything. You paid every extra expense above basic care for fourteen months of my hospitalization. And every penny of my rehab. Mom and Dad said you offered a blanket of money."

Jane lets out an embarrassed huff.

"No—really. Those were my mom's exact words. 'It's like she's giving us a blanket of money.' It covered everything, comforting and private. How can I ever repay you?"

"*Repay* me?" Jane gasps. "It's *my* fault you're in this position in the first place."

"No, it's not. It's the fault of the man who shot me."

"We keep coming back to this loop. Over and over. I feel guilty. You feel guilty. When are we both going to let this go?" Jane asks Lily.

"When he's caught," I say. They turn and look at me.

"When he's *dead*," Silas adds.

I didn't say it. He did. The boss has more leeway.

And now I'm not on the record with that incendiary statement.

Jane studies Lily, looking at her like her skin will magically display the answers to all the mysteries, like a tattoo that only shows when you watch it. "Romeo?" Jane asks.

Lily doesn't react.

But we all know.

"I've got calls in," Silas says, using a soothing voice, one designed to convey truth. "We're investigating."

"You've been doing that for more than two years," Jane reminds him.

"No amount of work is ever enough until the full picture is shown," he replies. "We never would have figured out the Monica Bosworth/El Brujo connection if you hadn't found the papers in Alice's personal effects."

"True," Jane concedes. "Speaking of which, the papers never end. I'm still going through everything."

"Why?" Lily asks, clearly relieved to have something other than Romeo to talk about.

"Donating Alice's papers to Yates University. Their archive wants them. I can't give them over until I've vetted everything."

"You can't hire someone to do that?"

Grief floods Jane's face. "I—I could. But this is a way to get one last feel of Alice. It's like I'm spending time with her, right here, when I read her papers. She's in there. It's my last little bit of her."

Lily takes Jane's hand in her own and squeezes. "I understand." She looks around, eyes dancing on one of the photos of Kelly. She brightens. "How is my little unicorn princess doing?"

Silas smiles. "Second grade now. Loves the weekly spelling bee. Mom's got her settled in back home. Kelly even has the same teacher I had, back in the Dark Ages. Mrs. Monticelli."

"You're not that old," Lily says to him with kindness. "I'm so, so glad she's doing well. What a sweetie."

"Kelly's been through the wringer. No kid should have to go through all that. Linda's made such a difference in her life," Jane adds. "It was bad enough when my mom died, but I was an adult. I can't imagine being five and..."

Lily puts her hand on Jane's shoulder, silent but soulful.

Compassion. Presence. Sweetness. All the pieces of her that make me want to get closer to her are here on display, in the aftermath of Lily being shot at.

She's taking this all better than I'd expected.

Moving to a safe house. Being sequestered. Not seeing her parents or siblings. Not having any of the creature comforts of home. Field agents lose their center sometimes, spending too long away from a place that signals their core identity.

Same with victims.

Two years ago, Jane started to unravel when we had to move her from place to place for her own safety.

Jane nods at Lily, then turns to the kitchen. "I'm going to put on a pot of coffee," she says.

"Do you want some help?" Lily asks, her voice tipping up. The question is less an offer and more a plea. *Please give me something to do,* that voice begs. *Please keep me busy,* that question implores.

Please give me purpose.

"Of course," Jane says, giving Lily a smile that makes it clear she understands completely. If anyone knows what it's like to be unmoored, it's Jane. She's been shot at, kidnapped, coerced into helping violent psychopaths in a deadly cat-and-mouse game.

She's been spat on, forced to leave public spaces, shamed, and wrongly accused. She's been falsely arrested and her apartment has been set on fire. Through it all, she's kept her humanity.

That much is on display now as she talks to Lily.

"Lindsay helped me sort some of the earlier boxes of Alice's papers," Jane explains as she wraps an arm around Lily's shoulders and directs her down a hallway. "You can take her place, even if you just keep me company. We started this ritual involving coffee." Jane's voice gets softer as they walk away, until finally I can't hear either woman at all.

"She's good," Silas says, smirking. "That was a smooth exit."

"Do you mean Jane or Lily?"

"Jane. She could tell I needed to talk to you alone."

"I've got a question for you, boss." I lean towards him, dropping my voice out of habit. "Why did you let Lily come here?"

Shorthand happens between people who know each other so well in the locus of a tightly knit community or experience. He knows damn well what I mean; I don't have to say it in any other way.

Silas nods, a series of brief up-and-down jerky movements that look like I've hit a nerve. "Jane insisted."

I shake my head. "You'd override that if you wanted to."

"I could've," he admits. "But I didn't."

"Because you want to observe Lily?"

"No. I mean, yes," he concedes, "but no, that wasn't the driving force. It was Jane."

"Her guilt's that bad?" I ask.

His eyebrows go up. "Yeah, it is."

"Bringing her here, though, puts the entire ranch at risk," I note.

"Leaving Jane in the coffee shop to be riddled with bullets by guys pretending to be gang members in the middle of some battleground is pretty damn risky, too, Duff."

He's right, but there's something about the ranch that makes me nervous. Raised in the city since Gran took me in when I was eleven, I'm the kind of guy who doesn't like wide-open spaces. Never liked being on assignment in them, hated doing overseas tour duty in them, and definitely don't like wide-open spaces inside my mind. When you don't know where the lines are drawn, that's where anarchy brews.

In quiet moments, though, I have to admit the real reason why I hate the country.

Because that's where we lived when my mom and dad died, and when my little brother disappeared.

"See anything of note?" Silas inquires, referring to the coffee-shop scene.

I shake myself out of the distant past. "No."

"Nothing?"

I know exactly what he's asking. Unfortunately, I have exactly nothing to give him. "Nothing out of the ordinary. Just looked exactly like what they set it up to look like–a gang-related shooting."

"Forensics is running tests," he tells me. "Nolan Corning and Monica Bosworth have been dead for almost two years. El Brujo's been dead even longer. All the major players who could have been part of this died long enough ago that their power networks should have unraveled. At least enough to slow all this down."

"It *has* slowed down," I argue.

"Not enough." His voice is so close to being despondent. I have to shake my head a little to make sure I actually heard what I heard. "None of these operations really fell apart," he says, expanding on his point. "New people move up. Power stays coalesced. You know how it works."

I nod. "Meet the new boss, same as the old boss."

He doesn't laugh. "We've got security at Lily's parents' house and at the shop, guys stationed at the school her brother and sister attend. Whoever is after her is good," he says to me, his voice mournful, soulful. Scratching his chin, he feels his own stubble and gives a wry grin.

"I hope you don't like sleep, Duff."

"Sir?"

"Because we're not getting much for the next few weeks."

"Weeks?"

He makes a huffing sound. "That may be conservative. I have no idea how long this is going to go on."

"We never really do. People who use death as an answer don't look at strategy or end game in the same way you and I do."

"Death can be a pretty powerful answer," he insists. A haunted look crosses over his eyes, the shine of a light against his cornea otherworldly and alien.

Furious whispering comes from down the hall behind the partly closed door. Silas hears it, too, and turns. His look is as perplexed as mine. Lily and Jane are hissing in harsh, pointed tones that imply they're fighting.

"What's going on back there?" Silas mumbles.

"Don't know."

The door opens and Jane walks out, red faced and livid. She is clutching a batch of papers in her hand. Light-blue writing paper, the kind used for sending airmail decades ago, is twisted in her hand. Her eyes are completely fixed on me. Silas might as well not even exist.

When a woman looks at you like that in the presence of her boyfriend, you're dead meat.

"When were you going to tell me?" she practically screams as she storms down the hallway and gets within inches of my face, Lily at her heels.

Lily holds up a handful of glossy photos, the kind of prints made in the 1980s and 1990s. The one on top shows two little blond kids.

I know that picture.

Oh, shit.

"Tell you what?" I ask, stalling, heart pounding until my ears ring. Where did that picture come from?

I know what she's going to throw in my face, but she'll have to toss it straight at me. I'm not making any mistakes. I'm not accidentally giving her any information.

Jane thrusts the blue papers towards me, the thin, onion feel of the dry parchment brushing against my knuckles. I feel a sharp pull and look down. A paper cut has split the skin above the second knuckle of my ring finger.

"When were you going to tell us, Duff?" she says, her voice so low that I can barely hear it. She is shaking with fury.

Lily points to the photo. "This is you?" Jumping between the photo and me, her eyes take in the contrast. My eyes are drawn to the port-wine stain on the littler kid's neck.

I'm the older kid. I look nothing like myself from twenty-three years ago.

Who does?

Jane blocks me in, inserting herself between me and Lily.

"When were you going to tell us you've been lying all along?"

CHAPTER 16

"You've known the Mogrett family for *decades*?" Jane demands. Her voice is shaking with anger. "I had to find a note from Alice explaining all of this. Notes, plural. She wrote to someone I don't know. But she never mailed these."

Her eyebrows knit as she looks at the paper, anger etched into her brow. "You've been *working* for Alice?"

"I—it—" I stammer. I *never* stammer. "It's not like that, Jane."

"Then what the hell is it like, Duff? Because it sure looks to me like you've been lying to everyone here for years. From this letter, it almost looks like you're part of some deep-state conspiracy—*and so was Alice*."

"No, no. It—" I'm caught off guard and so I falter. I falter more than I want to, because damn it, I'm shaking on the inside, too. "If you give me a chance to explain, I'll lay it all out for you."

Silas moves closer to Jane, protective.

"But I need to talk to you alone first," I tell her.

"Hell, no," Silas says under his breath.

I'd do the same in his shoes. I make a split-second decision and err on the side of confession.

They say it's good for the soul, so why not?

"If you read the documents, then you know that Alice hired

me. That Alice was behind the investigation into the Bosworths that's taken place for decades."

"You're not old enough to have been involved in this for decades," she says, looking at me like I'm crazy. I'm a guy who's just supposed to be wallpaper. I don't like being the center of attention.

"That's right," I tell her. "*Alice* has been investigating for decades. You knew that from the documents you went through. What you don't know is my role in all this."

"Then tell me," she insists. "How you were working directly for Alice Mogrett. How Drew thinks you're his guy, but you're not. Who are you, Seamus McDuff? Who are you *really*?"

I've spent the last nine months trying to convince Lily to tell me what she's been hiding all this time. And now irony smacks me upside the head.

Jane's demanding the same of me.

We all have a deep, dark secret. We all have a hidden self that slithers inside of us, doing everything it can to avoid detection. Sunlight is the great disinfectant, they say. Secrets lose their power when they're exposed to the sun. My secret is decades old.

It's older than me, stretching back to a time before I was born.

How do I share a secret that started before I even existed? And yet that's exactly what Jane's asking me to do. I give her the truth, because when you're in free fall, the closest thing to a net is a pair of eyes begging you to spill.

I've tried to be that net for Lily.

I never expected that Jane would be mine.

"My grandmother was a contemporary of Alice Mogrett."

Jane just blinks.

"She was the equivalent of a lady's maid to Alice when they were younger. Gran was about ten years older than Alice and came over here from Ireland when she was just fourteen. She came in through New York and found her way through a series of terrible domestic jobs into the household of the Mogretts. Alice was a wee thing back then, as Gran used to say. My Gran was nineteen and Alice was nine when she first started to work there. They were friends, if you could call it that. More of a nanny-and-charge relationship, but Alice trusted my Gran until the day Gran died."

Lily, Silas, and Jane just listen. The open space of their silence is deafening.

"Decades ago, when Alice began investigating Monica Bosworth and El Brujo–Ignatio Landau–she started with a private investigator. We all know about that. You've seen the documents. You *found* the documents, for God's sake, in Alice's papers."

I run one shaking hand over my head, rubbing hard, as if I could push the information out of my memory. "What you don't know is that about ten years ago, when I came back from my last combat mission, Alice recruited me."

"*Recruited* you? What do you mean?" Silas asks.

"It's complicated."

"It's always complicated, Duff. Just tell the truth," Jane interjects.

"The *truth* is complicated, Jane. You of all people should know that."

I get an eye roll.

The picture. Lily holds it up. I can barely look at it, a hole in my heart filling with black grief. "Is this the complication? The back of it just says Sean and Wy."

I wince. "Yeah. That's me."

"You said your name was Seamus," Jane notes.

I give her a cold look. "I've had lots of names."

"Are you Sean, or Wy?" Lily asks, nose crinkled in concentration.

"Sean."

"Alice had this in a folder with the letter about your work for her. You've known her since you were a little kid?" Jane asks in a tone that makes it clear she and Lily care about different issues.

"There's information I can share and there's information I'll take to my grave. Torture wouldn't get it out of me."

"Don't tempt me," Silas mutters.

"Here's what I *can* tell you. Alice asked me to work on digging into what she suspected about Nolan Corning, Ignatio Landau, and the benefactors of the Mosner Gallery of Art at Yates University. At the time, that was Monica Bosworth's parents–the Mosners–and Harry Bosworth himself."

"You're telling me that Alice was investigating *my father*?" Jane says, gaping.

"Yes, except not at the time. It's a web. I know it's a cliché, but the spider's web is woven in so many different patterns. Strong and yet almost invisible." I stare at her. "When Lindsay was attacked six years ago and you were part of it, you received a scholarship to Yates University."

"Sure. I had been there on scholarship already. That was explained to me before. My father set it all up."

"Your father set it all up, but Alice worked to get you there."

"Why?"

"Alice had a soft spot for fatherless young women. I don't know if it was because of Gran and Gran's loving care of her. I don't know if it's because Alice felt that her father had never been around, but she saw something in you. She also saw that your illegitimacy was at the heart of Monica Bosworth's manipulation on her path to the White House."

Jane flinches. "You mean Alice wanted to be close to me so that she could keep tabs on the Monica situation?"

"Yes and no," I admit. "It's a bit more than that. She really did love you once she got to know you."

"But you're saying that at first..." Jane says, blinking hard, processing everything. "It was just about getting me to Yates, getting me to where she could get to know me? Study me, learn more about me? Use me as a way of getting to Harry Bosworth and Monica?"

This is the part that causes actual pain. When you have to lay the truth on the line for someone.

"Yes," I admit. "That's how she began."

Jane looks like someone's kicked her in the gut. I can't blame her.

"So it was all a lie?"

"No," I correct her. "None of it was a lie. Alice saw that you were at the center of something very dangerous. And that Monica was brewing a series of lies designed to use you as a pawn. Alice wanted to step in and help."

"Why? Why would Alice be involved in any of this?"

I laugh. I can't help it. The sound comes out like a hiss. "You knew Alice. She had this righteous justice streak a mile wide. She also had the money to do whatever the hell she wanted. Combine those two, and you have a very dangerous person on your hands. Dangerous to people whose lives depend on convincing other people that reality is what *they* want it to be."

"Like Monica Bosworth," Jane whispers.

"Exactly like Monica Bosworth. She was ruthless and determined, and she sacrificed so much to position her husband so that he could become president."

"But in the end, it was all for nothing. She..." Jane's shoulders slump, the air slowly leaving her body. The vacant stare in her eyes as she tries to make sense of it all is familiar.

Too familiar.

"Why are you telling me this?" she demands.

"Because you're making me."

"Nobody *makes* you do anything, Duff."

"You found the evidence. I can't refute that."

"When everyone was pointing fingers about the shooting with Lily and everyone was trying to figure out who could've done it, so many people suggested that it was an inside job, Duff. That you did it. That you set the whole thing up to make it look like a weird error. That you came in and shot Lily on purpose."

"Oh, my God." We both turn to see Lily standing there, her hand over her mouth, eyes burning with accusation as I meet her gaze. "Did you set this whole thing up? Duff?" she asks, taking one step closer to me and then moving back on her heels.

"You know I didn't. You *said* I didn't," I tell her. "That day in the stairwell at my building. You said, 'No.'"

Jane's head whips violently back and forth between the two of us. "What are you guys talking about?"

I move closer to Lily. She doesn't step back. "You told me that I wasn't your shooter, Lily. Why would you question it now?"

"Why would *anyone* think that you had done it?" She looks at Jane as she asks the question, but I know I'm the target.

All three of us look at each other.

And then Silas steps out of the shadows and says one word: "Romeo."

CHAPTER 17

*J*ane's said it. Silas has said it. I've said it.

Lily still hasn't.

She's the one who counts.

"Of all people," Silas says to Jane, "you know what it's like to be set up. To have a secret cabal of people all working against you."

Pain fills her eyes.

"And to not know who's doing it or why they're doing it," he continues.

Her eyes flick to me. "Yes, I do. I think Romeo's setting Duff up."

Lily's face goes pale. "Setting him up for my shooting?"

"Yes. Not in terms of evidence. In terms of suspicion. This isn't about pinning the actual shooting on Duff. It's about innuendo and starting rumors that shake people's confidence. It's about manipulating and using people's psychology against them."

Silas looks at me hard. "You know exactly what I'm talking about. You're trained to do it."

"So are you," I tell him.

"I know," he nods. He looks at Jane and Lily. "Will you excuse us? We need to have a private conversation."

"There's nothing that you can tell Duff that you can't tell me,"

Jane insists. Lily takes a step closer to Jane, the two of them a united front.

Silas doubles down. "Actually, there is. You know if I could tell you, I would."

My blood runs cold, muscles tightening. Whatever he's about to tell me, it's not good.

"You swear?" Jane asks him.

"Of course," he says.

"I don't understand any of this," Lily gasps, her voice filled with frustration. "Two years ago, I was making unicorn arrangements for little girls in the flower shop where my parents raised me. And then one day I was shot because somebody thought I was *you*," she says, gesturing to Jane, who flinches, guilt that she doesn't deserve all over her face.

"I wake up and fourteen months of my life disappeared, I've got a giant scar on the back of my head, my bones are reknitting, and I get stuck with this guy," she points to me now, "living with me practically twenty-four/seven. My mom and dad are a wreck, my dad has a heart attack, and then when I'm finally getting better, someone tries to shoot me again. And now here I am in Texas, and you guys are all telling me that Romeo is the one who's responsible for all this?"

Her rant is good. I'll give her that.

I reach for her, grasping her shoulders, turning her towards me and looking down. I move closer until we're eye to eye, our faces inches away.

"None of this is a surprise to you, so just spit it out, Lily. Quit lying. You don't need to fake your amnesia anymore."

She holds her breath. So does Jane. Silas continues to inhale and exhale, just like I do. The body breathes autonomously and intentionally. It's one of the few systems in our physiology that does both. It's something we can control, and yet it's out of our control.

Just like love.

"It wasn't Duff," Lily finally says, looking down at the ground, unable to make eye contact with Jane, Silas, or me. "It wasn't Duff."

"You're sure?" Silas says.

"Of course I'm sure. I wouldn't say it if I weren't sure."

"You've said an awful lot of things that weren't true," I point out.

"Like what? I haven't lied about anything. I haven't told you anything that isn't true."

"It's what you *haven't* told us that's the untruth," I say to her. "Lies of omission are just as bad as lies of commission."

"That Irish grandmother of yours was Catholic, huh?" Jane says, her voice bitter.

"Yes." Might as well own up to it.

"I've never told anyone something that wasn't true." Lily looks at Silas. "Duff didn't do it."

"And you know who did it?"

This is the moment.

This is months' worth of patience, investigation, anticipation, and terror. Terror for Lily, at least. We're in Texas, surrounded by some of the best security in the country. Only the president of the United States has better.

But he also has Romeo, the guy who I now know pulled the trigger on Lily's defenseless back.

Lily breaks away from us and starts to pace, moving closer to the light, to Alice's large paintings, and then back towards us, her head shaking, her body moving rapidly with more symmetry than I'd expected.

She's recovered. Healed. But her memory hasn't.

Not that she doesn't have the memory. She does. But the trauma associated with that memory is still trapped inside her. I should know. I have my own, stretching back twenty-three years. The heat's off me for a few minutes, the memory of my mother, father, and brother being packed carefully back into the locked box where they live in me.

I'm focused on Lily now.

I have to be.

She's on the edge of an abyss, and if she jumps, she doesn't understand that there is a net. That we're the net.

How do I convince her?

It turns out, I don't have to.

It turns out, she has more courage than I ever anticipated.

Because Lily just goes ahead and *jumps*.

"If I tell you what I know," she says, hands in the air, flying, "then everything changes. If I tell you what I know, this cascade of ripples goes all the way out into my life. My mom, my dad, my brother, my sister, everything. Everything changes." Her fingers flow outward, mimicking water and waves on a pond.

"But, Lily," Jane says, grabbing her arm mid-pace and stopping her, compassion her chief feature. "If you tell us, we can stop him."

"How?" Lily says simply. "How can you stop someone who's hidden in plain sight all this time?"

"You've been holding this in all this time? You were paralyzed on that hospital bed almost two years ago and woke up one day, terrified to say a word? Why?" Jane challenges her.

"Why?" Lily yells. "*Why?* Because I woke up and he was there, standing right behind you!" She points at me, confirming what I already know.

She doesn't even have to say his name.

"God damn it. I am so stupid," I grunt.

Silas looks at me. I can tell from his face that he's thinking the same thing.

"Why didn't you tell anyone?" he asks.

"I just told you why I didn't tell anyone."

"You've been faking amnesia all these months, lying to neurologists, speech pathologists, psychiatrists, psychologists, everyone? Is this why you don't want to be in therapy? Because you couldn't hold the lie in with a trained professional?"

Lily looks at me. "I did it with you."

"Barely," I chide her. "I figured it out a long time ago."

"You did?"

"Yes."

"Why didn't *you* say something?"

"Because that's not how this works, Lily. I don't come to you and say, 'Even though you're faking amnesia to everyone here, I figured out that you really know who your killer is.'"

"He didn't kill me. He's my *shooter*."

"Are you really going to get nitpicky about semantics?"

This time, she's the one who marches up to me and grabs my shoulders, standing on tiptoe. Her pain is so hot, so blazing, I can feel it on my skin. She looks at me, laser-like, with a begging that makes me want to kidnap her and take her away to be safe.

"If I told you who it was, he was going to kill me. Then he was going to kill Mom, Dad, Gwennie, and Bowie. Then it would all be my fault."

"No," Jane says, but Lily holds up one hand, stopping her.

"I knew from the second I saw him in my room that I was dead if I 'remembered.'" Finger quotes accompany the word. "And now it looks like I'm dead even if I don't." She squeezes my shoulder. "You told me that the spider found in my hospital room was poisonous."

"What spider?" Silas asks.

I wince. "I'll tell you about that later."

"You never told them?" Lily's voice is filled with outrage.

"I kept it to myself," I admit.

"What's this about a poisonous spider?" Silas asks.

"There was a moment early in Lily's awakening when I found a spider crawling on her chest. I killed it. Turns out it was poisonous," I explain.

"That's because Romeo put it on me."

Jane and Silas gawk at her.

I smile, biting my inner cheek. Damn. Fooled again.

"I suspected," is all I say.

"You never told *me*!" Silas protests.

CHAPTER 18

*S*ilas's phone buzzes with a text. He looks down.

"It's Drew. He wants a meeting with us."

"Us?" I bristle. "I'm not leaving Lily here."

"He's already on the way. Says they just landed," Silas explains. Jane looks at him with surprise. "If Drew's willing to come here and leave Lindsay and Emma alone, it must be big. I suspect he views this place as more secure than..." he pauses, "...than the alternative."

"Which is? His own office back in California or the one in DC?"

Silas shrugs. "Either."

"It's all connected to Romeo, isn't it?" I ask, keeping my voice low, as if Lily and Jane shouldn't hear. Habit. Can't help it.

"That and more," is all he says. We're cryptic.

It comes with the job.

"Do we get to be in on this meeting?" Jane demands.

"What do you think?" Silas asks her.

"I think Drew is an egotistical control freak who—"

Silas shuts her up with a quick kiss.

"We'll be back soon."

"You're leaving now?" she says flustered. "You can't just kiss me like that and leave and not tell us what's going on."

One side of his mouth tips up. "Of course I can. Do it all the time."

"And I don't like it when you do it then, either!"

He lets out a long sigh.

"Just because Nolan Corning, Monica Bosworth, and El Brujo are dead doesn't mean this isn't a hydra. There are countless tentacles left in this mess. We don't know what's deep state. We don't know what's narco trafficking. We don't know what's garden-variety narcissistic manipulation. We don't know who is power hungry and who is out for even more." Frustration infuses every word coming out of Silas's mouth.

Meanwhile, I look at Lily, who's watching the whole thing with awe.

Silas gently takes Jane's elbow and turns her towards him. "I know you don't like this," he says softly. "I don't like it, either. But everything is on a need-to-know basis."

"Well, *I* need to know."

I can tell this is a well-worn argument between the two of them. Again, I look at Lily. It would be a well-worn argument between the two of us, too, if we were a couple.

A couple. The thought fills me with a grounded sense of desire, something I have no right to feel.

Bzzzz.

Lily jumps as if she's been stung by a bee. Reaching into her front pocket, she pulls her new phone out and looks down. "It's Mom," she says. "She wants to make sure I'm okay."

Jane smiles at her. "Your mom's pretty great."

"She really doesn't feel the same about you." Lily says bluntly.

"Yeah, I figured." Narrowing her eyes, Jane gives Silas an appraising look. "Fine. You can go."

"Glad to have your permission," he deadpans.

"But," Jane clarifies, her finger in his face. "I'm the one who is Drew's client."

"Only when it comes to Lily," Silas notes.

"Only when it comes to Lily," she concedes. "But anything related to Romeo is related to Lily." A shudder from her confirms it. "Therefore, Drew has to tell me what you know to the extent that... that he can tell me what you know."

"Fair enough." Silas concedes. "You realize that's what I was going to do all along," he adds.

"I know," Jane says brightly, perking up. "But sometimes you and Drew need to be told things a few times before they sink in."

"Only when it comes to control," I say breaking my silence.

They turn and look at me. Jane's amused. Silas is pissed.

"We don't pay you to editorialize, Duff." Silas says.

"Tell me what to do next, boss, and I'll keep my mouth shut."

He nods towards a doorway. We walk out into a long, tiled hallway with French doors leading to a small patio outside. I follow him, my heels smacking on the stones until we're a good distance away from the house.

He turns around and shakes his head as he looks at Alice's studio. "You know, the first time I came here," he starts, "Alice Mogrett held a gun on me."

"What?" I say. "She was a pistol," I add.

"Actually, it was a rifle. You know what I mean?" He grins at me.

"Yeah, I do."

"You knew her your whole life?" he asks, his inquiry more human than I'm used to.

I nod. "I did. My Gran talked about her a lot when I was a kid. And then I got home from my tours and went into private security, and after a while Alice found out. Hired me."

"Hired you to do what?" Silas asks, leaning in. I can tell by his demeanor that he already knows. There's no sense thinking I can keep the truth from him.

That's the other problem with what I do for a living. We all have secrets. Some of them are actually top secret and some of them are just embarrassing. Some of them are personal, some are professional. Some of them are silly and trivial, and some are deadly.

Facing a colleague who is as well-trained as you are in manipulation and control of the flow of information is hard. The problem is that you don't know what *they* know. And not knowing what they know means that sometimes you can feed them new information accidentally.

I *am* carrying a big secret. It has to do with Jane. It has to do with Lindsay Bosworth. It has to do with the events of just over six years ago, when Lindsay was gang raped by three people she thought were friends.

It has to do with a kind of rot that comes from trying to grow anything in deep soil that's already contaminated.

Two truths can be plausible at the same time. You can have deeply poisoned land that produces an abundance of food if cultivated. The problem is, taking a bite of the food can nourish–or it can destroy.

Not knowing what Silas knows about me, and not knowing what Silas knows about my mission with Alice, means that I have to parse my words carefully.

I can't say anything about my brother.

No one's come back to that picture yet. Once they do, this gets even more complicated.

I take three seconds to consider all this. We're at a standoff. He knows I'm hiding something, and *I* know that *he* knows I'm hiding something.

"Let's have it," he demands, hands on his hips, brow lowered, the power stance obvious. Unlike Drew, Silas is steadier, calmer. When guys like us play good cop/bad cop, Silas always plays the good cop. He's smart enough not to even bother with intimidation tactics or threats. This is a guy who lays it on the line and expects me to do the same in return.

Problem is, my secret involves his girlfriend.

That's when his calm, rational self is going to unravel.

"What do *you* know?" I ask him. "You have access to all of Alice's papers. You know more about me than I do."

"We knew from the start, when we hired you, that you were connected to Alice," Silas admits. "I didn't until recently but the people who vet all of our guys knew. It's why you were assigned here."

"I know," I tell him. "I was upfront about it."

"That was probably the only thing you've been upfront about." He stares me down, expecting me to crack.

Good luck with that.

"What exactly do you want to know, Silas?"

"What exactly do you want to tell me, Duff?"

"I don't want to tell you anything."

"And I want to know everything," he counters.

"I worked for Alice Mogrett. I work for you guys. That's really all you need to know."

"What did you do for Alice?"

"Security."

"But you did security for us."

"Sure."

"Why is there a picture of you and your little brother in Alice's files? A picture from twenty-three years ago."

Before I can form a cohesive answer that is plausible but still maintains my secret, we're interrupted.

A car pulls up, a black SUV like all of the other ones. Drew Foster gets out of the passenger seat and snaps the door shut. As he walks towards the house, a pissed-off look settles on his face.

That's his normal look.

Sunglasses cover intelligent eyes, which can be useful.

And intimidating.

"You," he says pointing at me. "We need to talk." This must be bad if he's come all the way to Texas from California and made a straight line for me.

I hold my arms out. "Shoot, boss."

If he weren't wearing sunglasses, I'd see the glare my words elicit.

Silas leads us to an outbuilding, one that's used mostly for grounds keeping. There's a small office in there with electricity and the basics. Silas unlocks the door and steps in first. We stand in a small circle, two against one.

"I don't believe a word out of Romeo Czaky's mouth," Drew informs me with a cold, clinical precision that I've come to admire.

I nod exactly once.

"But I can also tell you're not telling us the truth about *you*," he continues. "I did some digging. You started working for Alice Mogrett ten years ago."

"Yes."

"Why'd she bring you here?"

"Security."

"Dammit. Duff, why *did* she bring you here?"

"Security," I say again.

"And six years ago, what did she assign you to do?"

Ice water hits my spine. Shit. He's figured it out.

"Six years ago I was standing outside in the Texas dust and heat, just like always, helping Alice get to a plane to some art show. Or helping guests during their arrival and their stay at the ranch," I draw out.

"And what else?" he persists.

"I washed the cars, took care of invoicing, trained some of the new guys. You know. The standard."

Drew moves his left hand in circles as if he's waiting for me to finish what I'm doing. It's a mocking gesture. I get it. He's upset and I'm toying with him.

I'm toying with him to buy time.

I knew this day would come. I just didn't think I'd be facing Drew Foster over it.

Movement outside the window to my left catches my eye. Jane is walking next to Lily, the two of them on a path, the white rocks crunching beneath their feet.

I can't actually hear them. They're too far away, but my brain takes the imaginary sound and plants it there. Furtive glances towards our windows tell me that Jane knows exactly where we are. I suspect she knows exactly what we're talking about.

How much of that was theater back there, how much of it is theater right here, right now?

"You ever work on the El Brujo case?" Drew asks.

"No."

"But you knew who he was before this last case?"

"Sure, I'd heard of him. Everyone has."

"Alice Mogrett ever talk about El Brujo?"

113

"Not with me."

"Alice Mogrett ever talk about Nolan Corning?"

"Not with me."

"What *did* Alice talk about with you, Duff?"

"Mostly she ranted about needing a security team and how much she hated it."

"That include you?"

"No, sir. I was a special hire. You know that."

Drew leans in, eyes piercing. Commanding officers have a way about them. It must be in their blood. They hold their spines differently than the rest of us. Their legs move with a kind of authority few people possess. Doesn't matter if you're male or female. Doesn't matter if you're from the South or the North. Doesn't matter if you're fifth-generation military or a first-generation immigrant.

If you've got that in you, you can't hide it.

Drew Foster *definitely* can't hide it.

I suspect he can't turn it off, either.

His eyes turn deadly. "I'm going to ask this exactly once, Duff, and I expect a full, truthful answer: Did Alice Mogrett hire you to help set up the gang rape of my wife?"

CHAPTER 19

*S*ome questions must be answered with a question.

Like this one.

"Are you out of your fucking mind?" I respond, puffing up in fury, the accusation so big, so horrible, it cannot be allowed to stand. My shout comes at the exact moment that Jane storms in, Lily at her heels.

Great. An audience.

"Maybe I am," Drew says. "Maybe I'm out of my fucking mind knowing that one of my top security guys has been embroiled in a secret network right under my nose."

"It's not like that," I insist. Here I am on the defensive again. "I worked for Alice long before I worked for you," I start to explain.

"You've been double dipping?" His voice goes up in a mocking anger that I don't understand, but I know it's treacherous. "Lay every bit of it out for me now," he demands.

I look at Jane. Silas picks up on it. His eyes narrow. My pulse pounds in my temples. My mouth goes dry. Muscles twitch, readying for a fight.

Our physiology is designed to react to whatever data we are receiving. Emotions are data. I'm cornered. I have ways to get out, but they're all inelegant and inferior. Computers can process data at extraordinary speeds.

The human brain can, too.

Unfortunately, most of the processing takes place in parts of the brain that aren't revealed to me in this moment. They're all subterranean, and Drew Foster is nothing but surface right now.

Lily is watching and waiting along with Jane, who doesn't look at me directly, but instead blinks rapidly. Her gaze is fixed on a corner filled with light in the back of the room. She doesn't know it, but what Drew Foster is asking me to tell goes back to the very essence of who she is.

Who she's been forced to become.

"I had nothing to do with the events of six years ago, Drew."

"*Sir,*" he snaps.

"Excuse me?"

"It's 'sir' to you."

"Yes, sir," I spit out. Any other guy did that and I'd think he was being petty. Drew Foster is reminding me not just of my place in the pecking order, but that what's about to come out of my mouth is a security matter, not a personal one.

Given all of that, I know how high the stakes are. Alice gave me a mission. That mission is technically complete, but as Lily and Jane hold their space in the cloud of tension that envelops us, I realize the mission never had an endpoint.

At least, not the one Romeo has in mind.

Just like Lily, I've been holding a secret. It's a secret I can't tell. Not because the secret itself is dangerous to me. In that way, Lily and I differ.

I haven't been able to tell the secret because the lens through which so many people in–and outside of–this room view their lives would change so dramatically that the ripple effect would lead to a tsunami.

I'm not just some guy Alice Mogrett hired because of a connection with her former maid. On the surface, sure. But this one goes so, so deep.

Because I'm indirectly responsible for Harwell Bosworth becoming the president of the United States.

A guy like me isn't supposed to have that kind of power. And now, that same president's son-in-law is staring me in the face, his jaw clenched, nostrils flared, face red with fury, and he's demanding what he thinks is the truth.

Do I give it to him? There is a point where holding onto a secret has less value than revealing it. Knowing when that tipping point occurs can take a lifetime to master.

I don't have a lifetime.

Seconds pass as I weigh my options, Foster's body language increasingly aggressive.

"Duff," Jane asks, "what is it? Lay it out. Tell us." Her voice has more compassion than I have a right to expect. It derails me. Incoming data needs to be clean for robots to process it and act accordingly.

Emotional data is never clean. Never has been, never will be.

But it's not Jane who sets me askew. It's Lily. Every breath she takes as the tension thickens makes me feel more hopeless. The minute I admit what I've been hiding, I become Jane, Silas, and Drew's opponent. When you're on the other side of some-one, there's no room for trust. The sharp edges are how we survive. Lily hasn't been part of the mess that Drew and Lindsay and Jane have spent the last six years living.

But she's the biggest victim of it.

"You know that Alice had Monica Bosworth surveilled by a private investigator," I start, my words more halting than I want them to be. This is being *pulled* out of me. I have to give them enough truth to sound believable.

But I have to hold back *my* truth. They can't know why I'm really here.

Not yet.

Hopefully, not *ever*.

"And so," I continue, "once Alice connected so many of those dots, she decided to keep the surveillance going. Privately," I add, in case there's any ambiguity in Drew and Silas's minds. "It wasn't constant and it wasn't obvious. When I came out of Afghanistan, I needed a job. Gran helped me connect to Alice. It wasn't part of some grand conspiracy," I inform them. "It was just dumb luck."

"And?" Drew says, impatient.

"And, six years ago, Alice started to get reports hinting at a plot."

Jane's eyes go dark, her mouth tightening. "A plot?"

"There were rumors flying that one senator with power was unhappy with a California senator who wasn't playing ball when it came to some legislation that would help a notorious narco trafficker."

Lily looks utterly confused. "Can you guys break this down for me? I don't understand."

Jane freezes. "You're talking about Nolan Corning, Harry Bosworth, and El Brujo, aren't you, Duff?"

I nod. "Yeah."

Jane turns to Lily. "Monica Bosworth was tangled in a mess with El Brujo. Trying to work with him and Corning so she could boost Harry's power," she says slowly. "It was all a scandal that started right around the time that I was born."

"Oh, I know about that," Lily says. "But what does Duff have to do with any of this?"

"That's exactly what I want to know," Drew spits out. "What the hell did *you* have to do with the plot?"

"I had nothing to do with it. Not directly. But indirectly, Alice brought me in as the rumors began to fly." I steel myself and look Drew straight in the eye. How do you tell a man this? How do you tell *anyone* this?

His arms cross over his chest and I receive the deadly glare he's known for.

"Alice's private investigators were bringing scraps of information that didn't add up," I try to explain. "We didn't understand what we were learning and hearing."

"Just spit it out. Enough with the pussyfooting," Drew says.

"We knew less than thirty minutes before it happened what was about to happen to you and Lindsay and Jane. No, I had nothing to do with the gang rape of your wife. Alice Mogrett had nothing to do with the assault on you and Lindsay at the hands of John, Stellan, and Blaine." I pause and look at Jane. "Or the assault that almost happened to you."

Her eyelids close in misery, as if blocking out pain.

"We spent two weeks piecing together bits of evidence and figured it out." I look down at the ground, feeling something way too close to shame.

"But we figured it out too late to stop it, and for that I'm sorry, Drew."

CHAPTER 20

*D*ark, mesmerized eyes meet mine when I look at Jane, who is walking towards me with a slowness that isn't driven by fear.

It's driven by determination.

She knows.

She *knows*.

"After the rape," she starts, "when Lindsay was trapped in the mental institution by her parents, someone reached out to me to give me information I could feed her. To help her. And it did. But I never knew who that person was. He had an Irish accent. He was interviewed on the radio while I was being shamed in the media. His was the only voice defending me. Monica Bosworth turned everyone against me as part of her crazy plan. You were my informant, weren't you?"

Drew and Silas jerk as if electrocuted.

Squaring my shoulders, I fight instinct. I tell the secret.

"Yes."

I expect anger. I expect recrimination.

I don't see the slap coming.

Jane's hand moves faster than I expect, hitting me square on the cheek. Holding my space, I barely flinch. She's in the right. I deserve it.

A public humiliation is a small price to pay for what she perceives.

"That," she says, breathing hard, "is for lying to me all this time."

I nod, a jerky movement of acknowledgment on many levels.

She pulls her arm back again. I don't flinch.

"I should hit you a second time for using that Irish accent with me. Learned it from your grandma, huh?"

Silas steps forward and touches her arm, corralling an erratic animal without making it feel restrained. She looks at him.

"Did *you* know?"

"No."

She turns to Drew. "Did you?"

"Not until today." Unemotional eyes catch mine. "You're good."

"Don't know about that. But I do know how to fulfill a mission."

"Playing hide-and-seek with me while Lindsay was institutionalized and desperate for information was 'fulfilling a mission'?" Jane shouts.

"That's how Alice wanted it."

"You—*what*? Alice?"

"She spearheaded the whole thing."

"ALICE? *ALICE* wanted it that way?"

Lily steps into my space and touches my elbow. "I don't understand half of this. Could someone explain?"

Before I can speak, Drew beats me to it. "Six years ago, three men gang raped my wife, Lindsay. Abused me, too," Drew says, the words clinical. "It was all part of a political network designed to give a kingpin drug trafficker, one of the most powerful senators, and the Bosworths even more power. Monica Bosworth was behind it. She and a senate leader, Nolan Corning, thought they could use Harry Bosworth as a political pawn, each in completely different ways. Their plans backfired."

"Obviously," Lily murmurs. "They're both *dead*. Can't backfire worse than that."

He frowns at the interruption. "Now it turns out Alice

Mogrett hired Duff to feed Jane the information that Lindsay wanted while she was being held against her will in a mental institution by her parents."

Lily blinks rapidly, then turns to me. Her eyes go to my cheek, which burns from Jane's slap. "You gave Jane information to pass on to Lindsay?"

"Yes."

"Because Alice told you to?"

"Yes."

"Because she wanted to make sure Jane and Lindsay were safer?"

"Absolutely."

Lily gives Jane a raw look. "Then why did you slap Duff? He was on your side!"

"WHAT?" Jane screeches.

"He was! Sounds like you and Lindsay were victims, Alice knew it, and she was trying to protect you both. Duff was her tool."

"I wouldn't go that far," I protest.

"He was just a pawn!" Lily continues.

"Hey, now—I wasn't 'just' anything," I argue.

"You told me your goal is to be a robot. To carry out the client's mission at all costs. To make snap judgments in the moment and to protect the client. Alice was your client. She told you to give Jane information to pass on to Lindsay, right?"

"Yes."

"Then you were just a messenger boy!" Lily announces with glee.

Drew and Silas smother twin grins.

"I am far more than that, Lily," I growl.

"Then you're the mastermind? You were one of the bad guys?"

"Hell, no! I was working for Alice to protect Jane and Lindsay."

"Who? Who were you protecting them from?" Drew demands.

"At one point—you," I have to tell Drew.

He recoils, like buckshot hit him. Emotional buckshot, at any rate.

"Me?"

"We didn't know your role in the gang rape of Lindsay. In the first round of video, you just sat there. Until the second video was released, we didn't have all the evidence."

"*I* was the subject of an investigation by Alice Mogrett, too?"

"You all were," I have to admit. "All of you."

"Not me!" Lily pipes up.

"No, Lily. Not you. Alice was dead before then."

"Who else knew about this additional private investigation?" Silas asks sharply.

I know why he's asking.

"Monica Bosworth. Probably others."

Jane inhales sharply. Her words shake with pain. "Alice's death..."

Lily's eyes bulge. "You think Monica Bosworth killed Alice? My parents think Monica Bosworth is the one who tried to have *me* killed. Er, tried to have Jane killed, I mean."

"I think she's got her finger in a lot of the worst actions here," Drew says.

"Her *dead* finger," Jane grinds out, livid.

Drew should know. He's the one who killed his own mother-in-law. Now he's revered for saving Harry Bosworth. For rescuing the president of the United States from his deranged wife. At least, on the surface, that's the story: decorated war hero saves presidential-candidate father-in-law from homicidal mother-in-law.

From the inside, the story's way more complicated.

And I just made it even more so.

"We'll never know," Silas interrupts, sighing. "Autopsy results showed that Alice died of natural causes. She was ninety-two. At that age..."

"At that age, she still had plenty of life in her!" Jane interjects.

"No one's saying she didn't. Just pointing out the facts," he says to her in a soothing voice.

"The facts are that Duff lied. Alice lied. She befriended me when I was a student at Yates under false pretenses. I went into her class so devastated by the assault on Lindsay, from finding her naked and tied up and beaten. Alice was a balm for me. A safe haven. And now I'm learning she was intentionally searching for me? That our friendship wasn't organic? It was part of some investigation plot she had?"

"I don't think it was like that, Jane. Alice loved you," I say softly.

Jane's eyes are filled with pain.

Good.

The conversation took a turn I didn't expect. I'm being saved by throwing them all a bone—a damn big one. Telling them about Alice's role in uncovering the plot Monica Bosworth hatched to get her husband into the White House takes the heat off me.

Off what drove Alice to start this investigation in the first place.

"But not at first. At first I was her target."

"You were a person of interest."

"Because I was connected to Monica Bosworth! Damn it!" she shouts, throwing her hands up in the air. "Just when I think I'm done with wondering about people's motives, here we go again. Now I have to re-evaluate my entire relationship with Alice? The woman who gave me all this?" Her hands wave wildly around the room.

"She would never have made you her heir if she didn't love you," I say firmly.

"What about you?" Lily asks me kindly. "Did Alice make financial provisions for you?"

"Why would you ask that?" Drew questions her, giving me side eye.

She shrugs, but doesn't let go of my arm. "If Alice and Duff's grandma were that close, it makes sense."

I stiffen. "I can't answer that."

"Can't or won't?" Silas challenges.

"I did not directly benefit from Alice Mogrett's death," I declare.

"What was your grandmother's name?" Jane asks, opening the door to the detail I'm trying to hide. Gran's name is public knowledge. Jane will put it all together the minute I say it.

So I do.

"Eileen Mary Elizabeth Sweeney."

"Sweeney isn't your last name."

"She was my mother's mother."

"That's the name of a trust some of Alice's estate went into." She turns to Silas, confusion in her downturned brow. "It was a huge amount. The trust is for a charitable foundation that helps orphans who are raised by–" She gasps, big eyes meeting mine.

"What? Say it!" Drew demands.

"Their grandparents."

Lily squeezes my arm. "Oh, Duff."

"Don't 'oh, Duff' me. I'm fine."

"That's *my* line," Lily whispers.

"You worked for Alice all these years, knowing you weren't going to receive any of her inheritance, knowing she was creating a trust in honor of your grandmother?" Jane asks, agog.

"Yes."

Lily lets go of my arm and moves towards Drew with a hard look. "Then you guys need to stop."

"Stop?"

"Stop blaming Duff. Stop thinking Duff's bad. He's not."

Bad. Good. Lily still has an idealistic view of the world. Naïve, even. I'm surprised.

Still makes me smile.

Her stomach gurgles in the silent space between her and Drew. Jane scowls. "Let's eat." She pulls out her phone and starts talking to someone.

"Now?" Drew's eyebrows shoot up. "We're not having light dinner conversation."

"I don't know about you, but I need time to digest all this new information. And we can digest in other ways at the same time," Silas says, taking Jane's hand. We all move towards the door, making our way over to the guest house.

"Right," Drew continues under his breath. "Duff worked for

Alice. Alice figured out the attack on Lindsay just shy of it happening. Sent Duff to be Jane's informant to Lindsay." He shakes his head. "I still don't swallow it whole. What was Alice's purpose in digging into Monica Bosworth, of all people, in the first place?"

Jane rubs her nose, frowns, and looks at Drew. "Monica's family were the benefactors of the art gallery at Yates. The Mosners. Monica's maiden name."

"I know that. But what drives someone to hire a private investigator? A disagreement about how to run an art gallery doesn't provoke *that*."

I stay stoic. I keep my mouth shut. They're not wrong. Alice did start investigating Monica because of funding irregularities.

But she also did it for a very different reason. One that is personal to me.

And no one here can know *that* until I have no choice but to talk.

"I don't know," Jane replies, giving Silas an uncertain look.

"And here we have Duff, looking like a Soviet brick. You know more about all of this than you're letting on."

I engage my inner brick and look back with a soft gesture that says, *dunno*.

"But he doesn't profit from it."

"That's a stark way of putting it," Lily tells him.

"It's a stark topic. Can't sugarcoat it." He looks at her closely. I bristle. Then I realize what he's doing.

Lily yawns. Jane glares at Drew and says kindly, "Lily? You want to freshen up before dinner? Bathroom's down there and feel free to take a shower."

"Are we going anywhere tonight?" Lily asks.

We all shake our heads.

"Good," she says, relieved. "Then a long, hot shower sounds even better."

I guide Lily down the hall to the guest bathroom. I've spent enough time here to know the floor plan inside and out. I also know that Alice has extra sweatsuits and guest clothes, so Lily won't have a problem with the basics, though there might not be underwear for her. She turned down the offer to pack a bag when we were in California in favor of getting here faster.

I close my eyes and will myself to stop thinking about her walking around without underwear.

"Are you okay?" she asks me as we reach the bathroom.

"Me?" I can't keep the incredulity out of my voice. "What about you?"

"I'm sure it'll all hit me tomorrow like a ton of bricks. You, too."

"I'm used to getting shot at."

"I'm not," she says firmly, closing the door on me as if I've offended her. The shower water starts. I hear her opening and closing drawers and cabinets.

"Robes are on the back of the door," I call out. "Extra clothes in the wardrobe."

"Got it."

I'm sure she does.

I press my forehead against the closed door and give myself the luxury of a few ragged breaths to try to regain focus.

And then I turn towards the deepening conversation in the living room.

Because I'm on the job, after all.

And robots don't need to center themselves.

CHAPTER 21

*J*t's good to see Lily smile.

I can't call the dinner relaxing, but it's definitely a relief. Jane's kitchen staff manages to conjure up a feast on short notice.

Alice's studio isn't remotely formal. None of us *wants* formal. I'm half expecting to be kicked out of here at any moment. When that doesn't happen after the first ten minutes, I start to unclench.

Jane is still giving me little looks of distrust. We can understand why something happens without emotionally liking *that* it happened. That doesn't mean the process of accepting it into our bones is an easy one.

Or a quick one.

We're seated around a circular table. I have Lily to my left, Drew to my right, and Silas and Jane roughly across from me at ten o'clock and two o'clock. I'm staying quiet on purpose. It's not just good politics, and it's not just because I'm low man on the totem pole here. It's also because I'm vulnerable. Too much personal information about me has been revealed in a short period of time.

I've gone well over a decade without having this much revealed. It's jarring, leaving me unmoored. The rawness that comes from telling them the truth about my role with Alice destabilizes me. An internal shakiness that you couldn't feel if you touched my skin vibrates from within.

I don't like it.

I've always been able to identify with Lily and her wounds to understand her healing process, to grasp the subtle and not-so-subtle psychological developments that help her to reconstruct a self. What I didn't feel enough, though, was empathy.

Putting yourself in another person's shoes isn't just about imagining the body. We can create little movies inside our minds as mirror neurons give us the ability to imagine ourselves in someone else's place.

Going deep emotionally, though, is a skill set you can't develop. The building blocks have to be inherently in place. It's like fast-twitch muscles that allow athletes to go from great to Olympic level. You have it or you don't. And if you don't, you'll never develop it.

If you do, it's up to you to find a way to optimize it.

As we sit here eating, I focus on the food. Never underestimate the power of macronutrients in reestablishing stability and empathy, though there's no perfect ratio of protein to carbs to fats to give yourself an edge in that department.

I'm sitting here at the table, feeling all these feelings, when Lily taps my hand. She's freshly showered, her hair hanging in loose, wet waves around her face. Soaked through, the strands of her hair hang longer than they do when dry, giving her an even more wholesome look.

And covering the scar in the back of her skull.

She smiles at me. "You're a million miles away."

"No, ma'am," I tell her. "I'm right here, present and on duty."

"Must have a nice job if duty involves raclette." She looks at the hot stone in front of us with melted cheese and an assortment of meats and other foods.

I have to laugh. "It's a tough job, but someone has to do it."

"All of that back there," she says. "Does any of it have to do with—" she cuts her words off.

"With you?"

129

"With what he—" she reaches up and touches the back of her head, where the scar lives. "What he did to me."

"You can say his name. It's safe," I urge her.

"Romeo," she says softly. "What Romeo did to me."

It's my turn to reach for her hand. This time I take the initiative, threading my fingers through hers, our hands on display. Not on the table, but on her thigh. If anyone looked down, they could see.

I'm not hiding anymore.

"Thank you," I say to her.

She jolts and looks at me, scowling. "For what?"

"For trusting me."

"Anyone who would go through what you've gone through, Duff, is worth trusting."

"You didn't think that earlier today."

"No, I did."

"You did?"

"I've wanted to trust you since the moment I opened my eyes in that hospital bed."

"Why didn't you?"

"Because you were right there with him. I didn't know if you were working together."

Her openness is killing me. "Finally," I say, not realizing the words coming out of my mouth.

She looks away, a sad smile tickling her lips. "I was just thinking the same thing. Finally."

I squeeze her hand again. "You've been terrified for months."

"Yes," she confesses.

"What was the biggest concern you had? Aside from having him come back and finish the job?"

"Mom," she says. "Dad. Gwennie. Bowie."

"But he never directly threatened you," I clarify.

"No. He didn't have to. There was the spider. The note. The way he weaseled his way into Mom and Dad's life. Giving Gwennie rides." Her face scrunches up in anger, lips pursing. "I didn't even know about that until the other day. Sick bastard."

"He never did anything inappropriate to her, did he?" The thought fills me with rage.

"No, no, no. It was all psychological. You know, making himself look like such a good guy who was so concerned about me and about my family. It was all about manipulating my mother."

"What about Tom?" I ask, knowing the answer.

"I don't think Dad was as snowed by him. It was more the way he was always there, Duff. He didn't have to threaten me. His very presence was the threat. He found ways to turn everything upside down, until I reached a point where I didn't know which way was up."

"That's what we're trained to do, Lily. He was doing his job." Before she can protest, I hold up a hand and touch the edges of her lips with my fingers. "I'm not saying what he's been doing is right. Let me be perfectly clear. But I am saying this is what we're trained to do."

"Are you doing it to me now?" she demands.

"No."

"Don't ever do it to me. Do not ever make me the target of your manipulation. Not now, not ever again."

"Yes, ma'am," I answer.

"I'm not joking."

"Neither am I," I assure her. "Now that you've told me who your shooter was, I swear to you, Lily, I'll protect you from him."

"How can you? Look what happened at the coffee shop."

"Did you die?"

"No." She gestures at her body. "Do I look like I died?"

I don't want to tell her what I think about when I look at her.

Just then a bowl of fruit is set in front of me. The dinner plates have been cleared almost without my noticing.

"Hey!" Jane interrupts from across the table. "What are you two talking about?"

Lily blushes.

Jane starts laughing and takes a sip of her white wine. "Oh, I *see* what you two are talking about."

131

Lily quickly extracts her hand from mine. "No, no, it's nothing like that," she demurs.

Jane winks at her. "Okay, Lily. Sure."

The playful sarcasm is fun. I'd forgotten what fun is like. I observe plenty of it in the line of duty, but I never, ever participate in it.

"You're not off the hook yet, buddy," Silas says to me. "We have a lot of questions for you."

Drew gives him a sidelong glance. "Some of us have more questions than others."

"Yes, sir," I say to him. For some reason, that makes Lily and Jane burst out laughing until Jane yawns, the gesture long and sincere.

"I'm exhausted," she says, looking at Silas, "and I need a shower. It's been a long day."

"Of course it's been a long day," he says to her. "They're all long when someone's trying to kill you." A somber silence takes over, cutting through the jocularity of the previous minute. Exhaustion soaks in, my own tiredness hitting me.

Lily tips her head down, the ends of her hair starting to dry and curl up.

"I'm ready for bed," Jane says with a stretch. She puts her napkin on the table.

Drew stands, looks at me, and says, "We'll need to schedule a follow-up meeting. Confidential."

"That means we're not allowed to be there," Jane says to Lily in a mocking tone.

"Pretty sure I remember what the word 'confidential' means," Lily replies.

Silas stands next, Jane joining him, and soon all five of us are on our feet.

"Silas and I are going to use our room at the main house," Jane tells us. "Drew, are you spending the night?"

"No, I'm heading home to California," he says. "To Lindsay and the baby."

"How's she doing? And Emma?" Jane inquires. "I haven't talked to her lately."

"Good, good. Baby's fine. Lindsay's fine. Just have to keep her away from…" He gives Lily a look. "…this."

"From me?" she asks.

"No, not specifically you. Just…" Drew flicks his wrist. "…this."

"Duff, you can have the room on the other side of the hall. Lily, you already claimed one." Jane stifles another yawn. "I'll see you guys in the morning." She looks at me. "You know what to do."

Lily blushes again.

"Yes, ma'am," I tell Jane. Within a few seconds, we're alone, and Jane's right.

I do know what to do.

We walk down the hallway to the bedrooms. Sound is more acute. Scent is, too. She's become everything in the emptiness. We're in a secure location. I'm assigned to the bedroom across from hers. My job is to protect her in case the other layers of security fail. I'm the final line between life and death for her.

I'm her personal emergency brake.

"Duff, I…" she says before turning around, her face tipped up to me. The aura from the light behind her head makes her look like an angel, the moonlight dripping through the window glass, bathing her in glow. She breathes through her mouth, lips parted, eyes asking me before her words form.

I step into her space.

She steps into mine.

The point where two lines intersect can be plotted. And while calculus allows us to compute the area under a curve, math isn't enough for Lily's curves.

She tastes like sweet wine and strawberries as I kiss her, my mouth hungry, hands hungrier to taste the essence of this woman who nearly died yesterday. Nearly died on my watch, bullets flying, the president calling us in for a meeting that was almost as traumatic. I want to use my skin to take away her pain and suffering, to give her relief, to absorb it all because I can.

I can do it for her.

If she'll let me show her how.

Fantasy isn't part of my inner life but for the last few months, snippets of indulgence have broken through. Lily tastes like I imagined, fresh and deep, with an unwavering boldness that makes her rise up and press against me, urging me on. Her tongue moves against mine, fingertips at my waistband, pausing at my gun belt.

The reminder of violence, ever present.

The reminder of security, ever true.

I won't let anyone hurt her. Ever.

But will I let her hurt me? Because that's what is happening as her hands ride up my back, the still-damp tendrils of her hair brushing against the backs of my hands. I breathe so hard, so full, my body burning against her as she kisses me with an abandon I don't understand. How do you let loose like this when you've spent two years of your life constantly fighting?

The thought evaporates as her hands slip under my shirt and find my heat, direct skin contact so close to my cock turning me hard in an instant. Lily is taking what she wants, second by second.

And I'm standing here, ready to give.

Ready to feel the pain of pleasure.

The weight of my gun reminds me of my gritty job, the lingering grime of the day. With regret, I break the kiss, holding her in my arms, chest to chest, her puzzled, worried face shining up at me.

"I need a shower. It's late."

She pulls back. I cage her in.

"I'm not supposed to do this."

"I know."

"But I am."

"I noticed." A shy smile follows her words. She doesn't look away, though. Lily is one hundred percent here.

All in.

I want to be all in, too.

Pants tightening, I find myself at the mercy of her touch. "Let's sleep on this," I say, moving my arms from her body, feeling like we're racing at breakneck speed towards an emotion I can't define.

"Okay." Now she looks away. "I understand."

"Do you?"

"It's too much. You're letting yourself feel too much."

She *does* understand.

"How–how do you know?"

"Because," she says softly as she takes one step backward, then two, headed for her bedroom door, eyes on mine the entire time. "Because it's exactly how I feel right now, too, Sean."

Sean.

My heart jumps into my throat as she turns, her body eaten by the dark room, the door closing.

Click.

All I have is my breath. Her warmth is gone. Those words, though.

That last one.

Sean.

No one's called me Sean since Gran.

An older memory reaches through the decades and tugs at my heart as I walk into the bathroom, strip down fast, and crank up the shower to the hottest setting possible.

The spray feels nothing like Lily's hot, eager hands on me. I'm hard as granite and rush through the shower, avoiding touching myself because if I do, I'll explode.

Then again, maybe that's better.

Get it over with. Out of the way. Remove the hunger that makes me want to go into her bedroom right now and make love to her all night long. Bury myself in her. Breathe her in.

Control.

It has two edges, like a razor blade. Find the right place in the middle and you're golden.

Get too close to either edge and you bleed.

"Fuck," I groan, leaning my head against the tiled wall, letting the spray roll down my neck, my back, curling into rivulets around my ribs, pooling between my legs. I imagine the water is her skin, wet and soft beneath my touch.

That... doesn't help. Not one fucking bit.

I stare down at my erection.

It stares back like a drill sergeant screaming, "What do you think you're looking at?"

Except this isn't basic training.

This is my life.

Impulse management is my entire career. I always have my own under tight rein. Managing other people's baser natures is my job, too. People who sow chaos feel entitled to have their needs met instantly. Their wants are more important than anything else. Or any*one* else.

My job is to thwart them. Stop the assassin. Block the assaulter. Prevent the damage.

And never, ever have needs of my own.

Lily's cracking that wall, one look, one kiss–hell, one limp at a time. She just soldiers on, like me, moving forward.

Moving, period.

I rinse, shut the water off, and angrily towel myself dry, my damn cock a sentry between my legs, standing at attention. Turning in the direction of her bedroom, I stand like a dumbass, staring.

Like that'll make a damned bit of difference.

I realize, too late, I've forgotten my bag with clean clothes. The hooks on the back of the door are empty. Lily must have taken the only robe when she showered. Wrapping a towel around my naked body, I look in the mirror.

Wet, short brown hair.

One eye scarred, pulled down at the corner, same as it's been since I was eleven. I tell people it was hand-to-hand combat. I lie.

A grim frustration tinged with thumping blood.

The expression of a guy who is floating aimlessly in an abyss.

Sounds about right.

Opening the bathroom door, I march into the dark hallway, only to run into a soft, small body, my hands going out in defense, her scent in my nose before I realize who it is.

"Duff?" she whispers, pulling back. "Sorry. I just–oh."

Her eyes are on my towel.
Then she looks up.
All my impulses rush to the surface.
All my impulses are demanding their turn.
Now.

CHAPTER 22

a fair ringing, like a thousand tiny sleigh bells a hundred miles away, fills my ears. It's not a specific noise, but diffuse. It just is. Every machine in the background, from air purifiers to ice machines, adds to it, but they travel through the haze of bells, all jingling out of sync, all rushing towards us.

Towards the space between.

"Your–you–" The bathroom light is behind me, the hallway dark, so Lily has to stand close to see me. I could turn away. I could hide. Anger is a solid weapon in moments like this, too, when you want to deflect.

I don't want to deflect.

I stand my ground.

The pale line of her hand moves towards my bare chest, fingertips skimming the space over my heart. "These scars. So many scars, Duff. Sean. Where do they come from?" She takes my hand, tracing the lines on the back of it.

"Life."

"But–" Rappelling down, her fingers bounce on my skin, touching another scar, then another, my mind playing catch up to recall how they got there. Archives no one should have to curate rush out of old files inside my mind, remembering, reliving.

Preserving.

Moments like this shouldn't intersect with the past. Lily's touch is pure present.

Letting her touch me is my future.

She reaches my diaphragm, where a long, angry knife wound left its mark. Below it, to the right, is a grisly keloid, from shrapnel. All of my scars have names. Places. Scents. Feelings.

She's evoking every damn one.

One step forward and she's in my space, her leg brushing against the edge of my towel. There's another part of me she's about to touch, and it has feelings, too.

All of them rushing *up*.

"All of these are combat wounds?" she asks.

In a way, I think to myself, not ready to tell her the real story. "Right."

"And this?" I'm bent down, abs curling in, ready to explode on the spot but unable to move. Every second she touches me like this is torture, but it's ecstasy, too.

How do you fight that?

You don't.

On her tiptoes, she kisses the corner of my eye.

And just like that, we're on the other side of the hallway, my ass bare as my towel drops, her body flat against the wall and we're kissing, and she's moving up, knee bent, until she pivots.

If she weren't wearing pants, I'd be in her.

No words needed, we move as one entity into the bedroom, mouths on each other, kisses turning into one long, frantic release of months of pent-up uncertainty. Her mouth offers me access to all the parts of her I've wanted to get to know.

Invitations come in many forms, Lily's breasts pressed against my chest, her hair tangled in my fist, her tongue daring me to lick, suck, bite, lavish with endless strokes. All of it is breathless, breathtaking, enormous, and fucking *hot*.

Permission offered, I run my hands up under her t-shirt, finding no bra, no hesitation, no obstacles. Just her body, barely clothed, so close to mine.

Something in me roars.

I'm over her, on the bed, as I pull her shirt up, mouth on her belly before I can close my eyes. From the way she moves, I know she's taking off her shirt, making low sounds of pleasure as I move to her nipple, sucking it in with a flick of my tongue, the sweet taste of her incredible. My fingers catch her waistband just as her hands ride down my chest, my body moving up over hers.

I pause. We're panting, my mouth almost bruised by how hard we've kissed, the need to be closer to her too intense.

"I want this. I want you."

Melting, her body softens at my words. "I want you, too."

"You're sure?"

"Zero doubt."

"Sounds sure to me." All of the parts of me not touching her are cold, chilled.

"Because I am." Her hand clutches my ass, then lessens the hold, an appreciative caress coming next.

"You have any idea how long I've wanted to do this?"

Her mouth moves up in a grin, our eyes capturing each other. I'm looking down at her, shadows obscuring one side of her face, the effect alluring. Every time I inhale she joins me, our fused chests moving in tandem.

"Do you have any idea how long I've wanted to do this, Sean?"

Sean.

I close my eyes, throat tight, emotion threatening to spill out of me and all over her, pouring down the sides of the bed, under the door, out onto the front lawn and beyond, covering the world with a blanket of all that I am.

All that I was.

Lily slips out of her borrowed sweatpants, the release of more skin a raw, visceral joy. I kiss her again, this time slower, more deliberately, with the sense that we have more time.

This isn't some rushed encounter, snatched in between anything else.

This is us.

And that means beginning *right.*

Texas moonlight drips into the room through the small

cracks above the light-blocking curtains. The shutters are closed for security. The moon doesn't need a full view of us, but it can't help but steal a peek.

"Thank you," Lily whispers, making me jolt, shoulders rolling as I shift my weight and peer at her.

"For what?"

"Everything."

"That's... vague." I kiss her nose.

"You saved my life, Duff. Over and over.."

"It's my–"

No. I can't use that line any more.

"Your job?"

"My pleasure."

As she breathes, she moves me up, the force of oxygen replenishing her blood through her lungs an automatic response that is underrated. Rosy, sensitive nipples peak with my touch, her ribs distinct under my mouth. Feeling her breathe, the tactile sensation of experiencing that process first hand, so much of me touching so much of her, creates a circle of emotion between us that defies words.

Initiating a kiss, Lily rises up, pulling my shoulders, bringing me to her. I move against her, hips instinctively searching, her legs spreading.

I stop.

"Are you..." I start, fumbling for words, rational thought fading, "...on anything?"

"No." Regret fills her words. "You–you don't have a condom in your wallet?"

"It would have expired long ago."

"So, you haven't, um..."

I answer with a kiss that tells her what she's asking.

Nuzzling her neck, I whisper, "I guess we'll have to do everything but."

She tenses suddenly, her sharp gasp making me realize my error.

"That's 'but' with one T, Lily. Not two."

A throaty laugh, resonant and smoky, comes out of her, the sound going straight to my heart.

And places further south.

Her phone picks that moment to buzz.

"Ignore it," she groans, chest filling, a long sigh coming out of her as I lower my head, kissing her breast, making her breath stop in an instant.

Kissing a trail between her breasts, I reach her navel. My hands part her legs, fingers finding the warm, wet sanctuary where I know I can give.

Where having Lily receive pleasure is my only mission.

"Oh," she rasps as I move, seeking a pattern, a rhythm, whatever she likes.

Then I replace my fingers with my mouth.

I expect her to hesitate. To demur. Most women do. They feel embarrassed for wanting this, as if receiving pleasure from a tongue, from hands that slide under their bodies–pulling them forward, toward, around–is above and beyond.

What's above and beyond is the privilege of being given permission.

Lily, though, doesn't hold back. Doesn't question. Doesn't turn shy.

She moves closer to me.

Opening herself up, she runs her hands over my head, my short hair wet, the movement more sensitive than usual. Hips rising, she seeks me out. Guides me. I palm her ass and take pleasure in her taste, my erection straining hard against the bedcover, my body in a state of flow. Focused solely on her, I pour my soul into memorizing the curve and curl of her until I slip one, two fingers inside, wishing it were more.

Wishing I could fill her with me.

When I have condoms.

Next time.

There *will* be a next time.

"Oh, God," she moans above me, her fingers going tight, one hand on my shoulder now. My spare hand goes up to find hers, the clench mirroring what's going on inside her, walls clamping down as I work to make her come. Mastery takes time, but Lily makes it easy.

Her orgasm is right there, ripe and ready.

"I haven't–it's been so long–this is, *ohhh*." Splintering her words with a sharp inhale that cuts her voice in two, sliced by a rush of heat deep in her core, followed by her hips moving fast against me, I track her, giving her all the control as she comes and comes, free and unbidden by me.

With me.

How does she surrender like this?

How does she trust like this?

Wave after wave pours out of her until she stops, closing her thighs enough to send me a message. I stop. I wait.

I get ready to give her even more.

Rewinding time is outside of my wheelhouse. I can't do that.

But I can do more of *this*.

Abruptly, she stops me, pulling back with a smile, then moving to me, up on her knees like me.

The wrap of her hand around me makes me hiss.

"Your turn," she whispers, head going down as I bend back, palms flat, body more than ready.

My journey is much simpler, her hands and mouth bringing me straight to the edge, nearly tipping over in seconds. Ending this quickly isn't what I want, but she's so damn fine. The perfect storm of smarts, perseverance, toughness, and beauty.

And naked. Can't forget the gloriously naked part.

One hand's around the base of me, stroking up as her mouth performs sweet magic. The other hand moves up my abs, covering more terrain, just touching me for the sheer fact that she can.

I love that she can.

"Lily, I–" My pulse is between my legs now, in her mouth, clasped in her hand as I come, pouring myself into her, my own surprise turning to raw delight as she doesn't move, every nerve at attention, getting the full range of satisfaction. Her mouth is an indulgence, a refuge, a safe harbor–

It's fucking amazing.

When I'm done, I move over her, curling her body under mine, flat on her back.

She looks up at me like I'm the moon.

I kiss her like she's the stars, all of them in the universe, shining white-hot light just for me.

I bite her earlobe, half joking, half maniacal. "Next time, Lily, it won't be like that."

"Like what?"

"So fast."

Laughter moves her breasts against my bare chest. "No one's complaining here, Duff."

Call me Sean, I want to say, stung by the reversion.

But I don't.

We crawl under the covers and I yawn, close my eyes, reach for her–

and that's all I remember.

CHAPTER 23

I'm standing in front of The Thorn Poke, doing my job. The streets are loud, the shop at an intersection with a light. The walk signal changes, the beep-beep-beep of the auditory warning system a monotony I've learned to tune out.

My earpiece crackles, but no one speaks.

My cellphone weighs heavy on the cotton seam of my pants pocket. The heat is just strong enough to make me start to sweat under my suit. It's a warm day, but a dark, grey cloud forms off in the distance, above the treetops a few streets over. I see it only because it forms a thin, black line, too sharp and distinct to be a normal weather event.

Straightening as I stand on tiptoe, calves flexing, skin rolling into high alert, I arch my back and look everywhere. Peering towards the cloud, I watch as it balloons, puffing up like a marshmallow in a microwave, like dough rising, the yeast doing its job.

Clouds shouldn't do this.

Soon the sun is blocked out, darkness taking over, the dull grey making it hard to see. A cool breeze begins. The edges of the old, wood-framed windows of the flower shop start to rattle.

Oddly enough, I don't feel the breeze. The wind doesn't move the hair on my skin. My eyes aren't dry.

My body feels nothing.

A car drives along the road, staying on the right side of the yellow line. It stops at the red light, idling. Seconds pass as I look around. I *notice the normalcy, parsing distances between two objects, evaluating whether the surreal sense I experience is just me or something more.*

I look in the front window of The Thorn Poke, knowing full well that Lily and Jane are in the back. The perimeter has been checked, secured. I have no reason to think that today will be any different from other days.

Heightened security for Jane Borokov is my job. Vigilance is a tool, but when the dark cloud forms, funnels that move swiftly down into each and every car, prying open the lips of the drivers and entering them, turning people into dust and ash, I sprint into the flower shop, ripping the door off its hinges, the wind carrying it into the sky.

"Lily!" I scream. "Jane!"

But the room is empty, the flowers gone, arrangements vanished. The bank of coolers doesn't exist.

I'm in a warehouse the size of a football field. I look up. There's no ceiling.

It's all dark abyss.

No stars, no light.

No hope.

"Jane!" I shout again. No response.

When faced with the impossible, I do the only thing I can.

I run.

I run as the black clouds turn into hair, thick and wavy, flowing down like a curtain. The roots are the sky, the tendrils brushing against me dry and silky, like a spider's web.

I run through one more curtain until suddenly I'm back at The Thorn Poke, the greenery lush and abundant, the flowers vibrant and colorful. I take one step and squish into a puddle of viscous fluid, looking down, finding red. Lily's body is splayed on the floor, her head on the concrete, the blood pooling and congealing.

I look up. Romeo comes in through the side door. A single red rose petal peeks out under the black sole of his shoe. He looks at me without so much as a glance at the body on the floor and asks, "What happened to Jane?"

A chill covers my skin as I sit up in bed, heart pounding, the dream visceral and real. My breath comes out in small pants, spurts of air that purge me of unconscious emotion. It's as if the carbon dioxide in my lungs has a chemical component that attaches itself to feelings I just can't store anymore.

I breathe, and breathe, and *breathe*, as if Lily's life depends on it.

"Duff?" she says, sleepy, her body warm next to mine. I'm sitting up, naked. We're under the covers. She's in a t-shirt, the same one she put on after her shower. The one we took off together. How did it get back on her body?

Did I imagine the sex?

I sniff. No. I smell like her. Taste like her.

The only dream I had was that nightmare.

The sex was, thank God, very real.

She goes from confused to panicked in a space of time too quick for her to have any real sense of judgment.

"What's wrong?" she says in a high, reedy voice, so close to a shriek I can feel her vocal cords scraping against my inner ear.

"Nothing. It was just a dream. Go back to sleep."

"You're shaking," she says, touching my bicep. I haven't had a woman touch my bare skin in a very long time, but I know damn well my reaction has nothing to do with that.

"I'm just cold," I lie.

"Then get back under the covers," she urges me.

The familiarity throws me off. The dream was too weird. The surprise of waking up with her in bed with me, the vulnerability of last night's conversation, it all mixes together to leave me too unbounded.

I need clear edges around all of the pieces of me.

"Duff," she says softly. "You asked me to trust you." Searching eyes meet mine. "I need you to do the same."

"It was just a dream," I insist, the repetition a confession. I know it, and she knows it. But with Lily, all those hard edges are blurring in a way that feels freeing.

I fight it. I do. If I were one unified man whose base components were all in agreement about the path forward, I could click into robot mode and shut this conversation down.

But I'm not.

A drop of sweat starts a lonely journey from the base of my

collarbone down my chest, pooling at my belly button. Lily watches it, entranced.

The sound of our breath is all I can hear. If all of the pieces of me were in agreement, I wouldn't be here, half naked, sweating, debating whether to tell her what my subconscious just reminded me of.

"I can't believe I missed it," I admit. Feels like I just handed her my brain, pulsing and dripping.

Or maybe that's my heart.

"Missed what?"

She sits up, but stops touching me, leaning forward on her knees, giving me her full attention. Her hair must have still been a little damp when she fell asleep. It's flat against one side of her head, curled and disheveled on the other. The rumpled look suits her.

For some reason it makes it easier to talk.

"I had a dream about Romeo and you."

"Romeo and me? What about us?"

"About the day he shot you."

"*Oh.*"

That single syllable has more emotion in it than a thousand words.

"What about that day? You dreamt about it?"

"I... yes." My words are halting. "It was a combination of a regular crazy dream and reality."

"You remembered something that you'd forgotten?" she asks.

"Something like that."

"What was it?"

"I–I'm not sure it's important," I stammer. "But at the end of the dream we were at The Thorn Poke. You were on the ground. You had just been shot. Romeo came running in from the side door." I close my eyes and remember the moment. "He ran in through the side door, and the first words out of his mouth were 'What happened to Jane?'"

"And?" she asks, clearly expecting more out of me.

"Why would he ask what happened to Jane when it was you on the floor and Jane was behind us, screaming?"

Her eyes go wide. "Oh, God."

I beat my fist against the mattress twice. Damn it, I missed it. I've known that all this time.

I close my eyes and remember what Romeo looked like that day. "He had a rose petal on the bottom of his shoe. How the hell did he get a rose petal if he was on his way for a shift change, coming in to work?"

"We don't do roses through the side door," she says to me. "Only through the back."

"Exactly. This is what I mean. I missed it. I missed all of this."

"Duff, it's… it's… they're small details."

"The details *matter*. Details are life and death in this business, and I missed these two."

"You had no reason to suspect him."

"Lily, I have *every* reason to suspect everybody. That's how this life works."

"I thought that's how this business works."

"Business, life. They're all the same."

"Not for me," she says in a small voice. Her fingertips graze the stubble on my cheek. "You don't have to live this way, Sean. No one does." Our eyes lock. I see a world in hers I rejected a long time ago.

A world where I'm connected to people.

"I like my life just fine," I lie. That statement wasn't a lie until I got to know her, though.

"Do you? Which life?"

"What?"

"The life with me in it? Or the life without me?"

She's touching me, our gazes locked. A gift is an offering. We take a piece of ourselves–time, money, emotion–and thrust it forward, into the space of the person who takes it.

We hope it connects us.

Her words are a gift. The chance she takes is the offering. What she's giving me is the opportunity to be with her. To share myself with her.

To stop being a wall.

She's finding my door, knocking on it, and asking for an invitation.

"Come here," I say softly, the words a gift, too.

Lily's arms wrap around me, the closeness its own reward. We drift off to sleep entwined in each other. Words don't matter.

Being present together does.

CHAPTER 24

The gym is the best place to get out all your ugly emotions. Especially when it's your job not to have any of them.

We're back in California, Alice Mogrett's ranch a recent memory. Once Drew and Silas declared that the ranch wasn't any better for Lily in terms of safety and comfort, and after Bee made such a stink about Lily's medical care, we decided to bring her back.

Rhonda is working with her on a balance ball. Other than us, the place is deserted. Clem's here, but he doesn't really count.

The goal is for Lily to be able to rest one knee on the large therapy ball and lift five-pound weights with her arms. So far, so good, as I watch them from across the gym in the squat cage, where all I care about is blowing my thighs to smithereens.

Muscles are works of art, but they are also finely tuned machines of science. Enzymes, hormones, and proteins all combine with kinetics to build a tool that can be used at will or an asset that can be destroyed by atrophy and abuse.

Neutrality has its costs.

Never using a tool–for good or evil–means that you never take a risk. Walking right on the line gives you a great deal of safety, but a very narrow existence.

Sweat pours off me like a guilt shower. It feels good. Some baptisms come when we least expect them.

It's been three days since all the reveals happened back at the ranch. Drew and Silas have initiated deeper investigations, calling on undercover agents and field operatives, and calling in favors.

No one knows much about Romeo. That's the whole point. We know that there's no record of his birth. He's in his early thirties. He says he's from Romania. His accent gives that away, which means he didn't leave the country until he was older, probably shortly after puberty set in.

On the other hand, accents can be trained into us for subterfuge. There's no paper trail on him: he's stateless. That's a term of art, one that we use in the field for someone without a document trail.

Stateless operatives are highly coveted. My particular interest in all of this–and the entire reason Alice invited me to work for her–has to do with the stateless.

Romeo has been a person of interest to me since long before this mess. Let's just say it's personal.

He served in the army, which means someone very high up had plans for him, because how do you serve if you don't exist?

Now he's working at the White House, hired specifically for that role by President Bosworth, who is either a damn fool or a cunning player at a level way beyond anything Drew has imagined.

"Yo, Duff!" Rhonda shouts, pitching a lightweight ball my way. I jump and catch it, my t-shirt sticking to my sweat-covered belly.

"Damn, Duff!" old Clem shouts. "Some guys got a six pack. A few got an eight pack. You got a fourteen pack."

I laugh at him. "How 'bout I give you four of those?"

"Make it six, and you got a deal."

The guy's eyes have been turning yellower with every encounter we have at the gym. Rhonda doesn't say much about him, but I know men like that. I've seen them at the VA hospital.

They come, they stay, they get their treatment, and then one day they're just gone.

Guys like Clem make me question my life choices. There's no room for ambiguity and regret in what I do.

There's no room for a life, either.

Lily's wrong about that, what she said back at the ranch three nights ago. Logically, I know she's wrong. I feel it in my bones, but my heart and my bones don't agree on this one, and I'm not willing to turn my heart off.

Not when it's finally been activated.

John, the physician's assistant who has worked with Lily the most since her discharge from the hospital, comes into the room, his nose wrinkling at the scent. A hot PT room with sweaty patients smells nothing like a clinical ICU ward.

I grab a towel, wipe my face, and join the group where Lily, Rhonda, and John stand in a horseshoe-shaped curl. I catch the end of John's words as I get closer.

"...we're worried about stroke at this point," he says, the words making my already rapid heartbeat zoom through the roof.

"Is it bad?" Lily asks.

"No." He shakes his head. "You're statistically at no greater risk of stroke than any other traumatic brain injury patient," he says, laying out his words in a measured tone. "It's not that you are at greater risk, it's just that you are *at* risk. I want to stress this as you two go forward and push for more function," he says, pointedly looking at Rhonda.

"I don't want to back off," Lily interjects. "I'm still not fully functional."

"You're damn close," I argue.

John gives me a look that makes it clear he doesn't understand what her security guy is doing in the middle of this conversation.

I don't care what John thinks.

"I'm not telling you to stop," he stresses, focusing his attention on Lily. "I'm just telling you we have to take the stroke risk into account. You've passed the first three-month stretch, which is the most critical for strokes, and you *had* strokes during that period. I realize you weren't aware of it," he continues, holding up one finger as if he anticipates arguments from her. "So that's good."

She nods, waiting for more.

"But, Lily, you were in bed for fourteen months. You had some of the best care of any of my patients, with PT and OT coming regularly. You were exercised frequently. You were given top-of-the-line medical treatment. You're on the bleeding edge of any patient that any of the experienced neurologists and neurosurgeons have seen at this hospital."

Lily rolls her eyes. "I know. I've heard this before."

"You may have heard it before," John says, kindly but firmly, "but you need to hear *this* now. Pushing too hard in here could end up setting you back. It's the same with stress. You cannot live a stressful life."

Lily snorts. "I don't know if anybody made you aware, John, but I was shot at *again*."

"I heard," he says, sighing. "I'm sorry."

"I'm sorry, too," she shoots back. "I'm sorry I can't live a life without stress."

Her eyes meet mine. I know exactly what she's thinking. Hiding the secret about Romeo was a source of unimaginable stress. Thank God I can carry it *with* her now.

Maybe even *for* her.

"You can't control people shooting at you," John continues, "but you can control your other risk factors for stress and therefore for stroke, blood clots, and other vascular issues."

"Bottom line," Rhonda says before Lily can object, "We just need to pace you."

"Yes," John says, relieved to have someone who understands.

"I'm tired of being paced," Lily says with a near snarl. Her eyes jump to mine and then flit away. Something about her demeanor makes me sit up and pay attention on a different level. There's something about *me* that is affecting her reaction to all of this.

"What is it? I can walk," she says to John, a plaintive tone coming into her voice. "I can't run yet, but I'm close. I'm much weaker on the left side, but I'm getting better. I can smile symmetrically if I try really hard. My hair," she says, reaching up to stroke it, "has gotten long enough now to cover the scar. I just want to be normal."

I brush my fingertips against my own scar at the base of my eye. "Yeah," I say to her as she turns and acknowledges me. "You wouldn't want to go through life looking like this."

"That's not what I meant," she says.

"Right," I tell her roughly. "But I don't give a rat's ass what anyone thinks about me and my scars, Lily. You shouldn't, either."

"It's not about the scars. It's about me claiming my life. It's about not letting that fucker win."

"*That* I understand," John says to her before anyone else can react. "But his goal was to kill you. A stroke could kill you, too."

A long sigh flows out of her. "Got it," she says. "Message received." Turning to Rhonda, she asks in a subdued voice, "Okay, what do we do now?"

Rhonda hands her a bottle of water. "We hydrate."

An hour later, I have a very quiet Lily in the car next to me, half asleep, turned away. She's not sleepy because she's tired. She's sleepy because we can only handle so much.

Strokes. John brought up strokes.

A red light gives me a chance to idle and look at her.

I spend all day with her, and it never feels like enough. What happened at the ranch was a start. The longer I'm with her, the more I want a middle. I want an end.

I want it all.

A honk from behind startles me. My foot presses the accelerator a little too fast, making the car jump forward. Lily makes a sound of surprise, then settles back down, head to the right, eyes closed.

I drive to her house.

I make my mind blank.

When we pull up to the front of her place, her mom and dad

are in the front yard, raking. Lily looks at me with trepidation. She doesn't want to cross the streams.

"I'll stay here," I tell her, giving her an out.

Her hand covers mine. No one can see the physical contact from a distance.

"Thank you," she says.

"For what?"

"For you."

The door opens. Her skin leaves mine. Lily closes the car door and walks away, limping slightly.

I pull out my private phone, the burner I'm not supposed to have.

And I get to work, the vision of her limp fueling my determination.

Where do you go when you need to dig up information on someone who is untraceable?

I can access Romeo Czaky's official record. That's easy. It's all clean and bright. Nothing to see here, folks. Nothing outstanding, nothing awful. Just a good ex-soldier doing his job, coming home and working security.

Just like me.

Scratch the surface, though, and there's more.

Just like me.

I can find my way around code, but I'm no hacker. Definitely not a cracker. I know my limits. I know when I'm outclassed.

What I also know is how to find people who are experts. Move one step above my abilities. And then leverage them to keep on moving up until I find what I need.

I've put out feelers. The darknet is all about money. People get off on being outlaws. Leveraging that is easy. Enough cash and some ego strokes and you can move mountains.

Move a mountain and sunlight exposes something formerly buried.

One problem with the darknet is knowing the difference between the operatives and the agents posing as operatives, though. Being an operative myself makes it slightly easier to catch.

Information like this doesn't get sent to you in a Gmail attachment. No one stores this on a shared drive. The irony of using the darknet is this: the information you find there is the kind you need a face-to-face meeting to distribute.

High tech meets low brow.

No fucking way am I meeting some rando from the creepiest edges of the internet in a back alley in San Diego. Not crossing the border into Tijuana for a handshake and an exchange, either. What I need to know can be found with a few inquiries. Confirming my suspicions won't take much.

And speaking of Tijuana... I can't stop thinking about El Brujo.

The drug kingpin died years ago. I know the truth. Mark Paulson's brother's girlfriend did it, a woman who'd been kidnapped and sold to El Brujo himself as a sex slave. She escaped, and when El Brujo's guys kidnapped more women, she helped rescue two of them. Shot the guy straight in the face.

Paulson took credit to give her an out.

Most guys take credit to make themselves look good.

Being invisible means acting in ways that most people interpret one way, but you know are motivated by a completely different set of intentions.

Nothing is ever what people assume.

That's where the real traction kicks in.

Online rabbitholes are funny things. One search leads to another. For the average person, this means finding your way to YouTube. Watching silly videos. Reading about conspiracies. Finding the new diet fad or vitamin deficiency that can be cured by some new product.

For me, it's about connecting the details that keep me up at night.

Tijuana.

El Brujo.

Romeo.

Why do those three *feel* connected?

Robots can't have feelings.

But we can analyze.

Bzzz.

A text from Lily.

Sorry I was a pain today. Will I see you tomorrow?

I'm on duty. Six a.m., I reply.

Tijuana.

El Brujo.

Romeo.

Rose petal.

I jerk in my seat. Rose petal? What made me think of that?

Impulse makes me do a quick search: "el brujo tijuana rose petal."

I expect nothing.

I get more than I bargained for. A connection I never considered.

Son of a bitch.

CHAPTER 25

"Absolutely not," I tell her, holding back my laugh at the ridiculous request. It's five minutes after six in the morning and we're in her kitchen, whispering furiously, crappy coffee brewing in her parents' machine while I ignore the smell as best I can.

"I didn't ask your permission," Lily says, lacing her hiking boots with a tug of frustration.

"Good, because you weren't gonna get it."

"I need forest therapy," she says, as if that's a thing. "Lush greenery. I need to spend time in nature. I can't keep living like this."

"Like what?"

"My life is an endless loop of fighting with my mom, going to doctors and physical therapists, and spending too much time in my own head."

I can't argue with her on that. She's right. "Where do you want to go?"

She names a state park an hour or so away.

"If you want to be one with nature," I point out, "the ocean is a lot closer. Why not go there? Everyone here loves the ocean. It's what Southern Californians do."

She laughs. "Only someone who isn't from around here would say that, Duff."

"I'm from Philly." I hold my hands up, palms facing the sky. I'm stalling. If she were a little more observant, she'd notice that.

She has no idea what she's asking of me.

A simple hike in the woods feels like death to me. Cities are safe. Suburbs are safe. Nature? Wilderness? That's where people die. Disappear.

Like my mother and father.

Like my brother.

Like me–almost.

"Everyone does love the ocean," she says, oblivious to what I'm going through on the inside. That's fine. I can keep it under control.

I grunt in response to her words.

She ignores me and continues. "Including me. But that's not what I want. I want to go out and be surrounded by greenery. Go for a hike up a mountain. I want to be in a place far away from here, where all I have to do is move and be and not think all the time."

"How important is this to you?" The minute the words are out of my mouth, I realize I've already lost the argument.

She beams. It's a smug, satisfied grin that says she knows, too.

"Let me talk to Gentian," I say grudgingly. "We'll clear the area and get a team."

"A team?" Alarm fills her features. "What do you mean, *a team?*"

"You think we're going on a hike in the middle of nowhere with just me to protect you?"

"That was my idea," she says slowly. "I don't think that some-one's going to come out of nowhere in the woods and try to..." Each word comes out of her mouth haltingly, stunned, until finally she winds down and stares at me in silence. "There's no escape, is there?" she moans, the end of her question a whimper.

"No," I say, hating the word as it rolls up from my gut, across my vocal cords, and off the tip of my tongue to hang there between us. That one word, "No." Lily hears too many *no*'s in her life. I hate being one of them.

At least this *no* is a truth, as hard as it is to accept.

"I still want the hike," she says, angry and irritated. It covers for her fear, a deep fear that I'm starting to worry isn't going away. People shouldn't have to live from a core point of fear, but they do.

Many of us do.

I just let out a long, resigned sigh.

"Then it's settled," she says, as if that alone would make it so.

"Nothing's settled here, Lily."

"We're going on a hike, Duff."

"Let me check in with Silas and Drew."

Her hands move to my shoulders, her face tipping up with a look that's half plea and half demand. "I need this, Sean."

That's better. Hearing my real name from her lips feels better than it should.

"I know you do. I'll make it happen." My ears sharpen, listening for any sound of Bee, Tom, Gwennie, or Bowie. It's one thing for Silas and Jane to know that Lily and I have crossed a line from professional to personal. It's not as if they have any room to criticize.

Bee would have my head if she knew.

Three hours later, we pull into the national park entrance. Silas assigned Ralph and another guy, Justin, to stay on the trail with us, but a quarter mile or so behind.

Lily insisted on the privacy.

I have to admit, the idea of spending hours alone with her in that kind of peaceful environment is appealing. It's also vulnerable. If someone wants to take her out, it would be easy. Wide-open spaces are any security guy's nightmare. They're second to large crowds, but this is one request that isn't just a request.

It's Lily's way of reclaiming a part of her life.

We get out of the car. The standard black SUV I expected to see is waiting in the parking area, and Ralph and Justin emerge. Unlike our normal uniform for work, they're not wearing suits. Instead, they're dressed for a hike, like me. The four of us look like something out of an outdoor sports magazine, which is fine. It means we blend in with all the other folks.

There are more people here than I'd imagined. The more, the better. Romeo's not stupid. There's no way he'd use a gun in an environment like this. Too many witnesses. The authorities would be here instantly.

It's paradoxical, because what happened back at the coffee shop was about as laden with witnesses as you can get, but that was a set up.

That was theater.

We grab maps from a park ranger's station, and I start to unclench a little. This is pure hiking, no rock climbing. Lily wants to go into the woods, the trees rising like skyscrapers with roots. We each have a backpack, and I'm wearing a water vest, a half gallon evenly distributed across my chest. It's a handy disguise for my gun, too. There's no way we'll suffer from a lack of provisions.

"How far up the trail do you want to go?" she asks me.

I put my hand over my heart. "I have a choice here?" I'm looking at the weather app on my phone.

She smiles. "I get to make all decisions?" she asks in a playful tone.

"You're the one in charge."

"Music to my ears, Duff," she says, nudging my elbow, and with that, she takes off at a fast clip ahead of me, leaving a beautiful view of her ass.

"There's a strong chance of rain in an hour or so," I warn her.

"Walking in the rain is fun," she calls back.

I groan.

Ralph and Justin hold back, fading away into a smattering of people behind us, until finally they're far enough away for me to know that we have some privacy but close enough to know that if the shit hits the fan, we're covered. They'll react in seconds.

Lulled by the greenery as we walk up the rocky path, I have to give Lily credit. This is its own kind of peace. Silence is our language as we take step after step, muscles working in ways you just can't manage in daily urban life.

The evergreens stretch high into the sky, some impossibly thin, like spires, others fat as if pregnant. The vaulted ceiling of greenery reminds me of the old cathedrals Gran loved so much, the songs from Mass soaring into the wood and stone and stained glass.

"It's almost holy," she says to me with a reverence that makes me ache.

I watch her profile as we move together, the path widening enough to walk in tandem. "It is," I say, staring at her.

Her hand slips out of her left pocket and reaches for mine, our fingers entwining.

I'm not supposed to do this, I think to myself. If Ralph or Justin reported this back, there would be an official paper trail. Mike didn't say a word about our kiss in the car. I know Silas overlooked what little he saw at the ranch, an unspoken agreement between us, tenuous and fragile.

But this? Being caught by some low-level grunts in the system and reported? It could force Drew to act. I squeeze her hand, and then I hold even firmer because suddenly, I don't care about being reported. Not anymore.

As romantic as holding hands is, it's hard to walk on a hiking trail that climbs at a steeper rate as we go along. She breaks the contact first, edging slightly ahead of me at my urging. I want her in front, but I want her close. Threats come when you least expect them.

Unfortunately, there's no good way for me to be in all places at all times. If I could, I wouldn't be human.

In fact, I'm not supposed to be quite human in this world, but Lily is changing all of that.

"Look!" she says, pointing into the woods. "A stream."

"Don't see many of those around here," I say, marveling at the look of lush ground cover down a small hill to our left. Years of drought in this part of the country have made the brown landscape around our area of Southern California the default view. I can go months without seeing anything that isn't artificially watered. Like most people here, I've come to associate greenery with wealth, because you have to have money to be able to afford the bills that come from maintaining landscaping in the face of severe water shortages.

Out here, though, it's different. It's nature. No one's paying for this. No one's using this as a status symbol.

I crash into Lily, who has stopped to take in the scenery, hips slamming into her ass, my hands going instinctively to her elbows, our bodies pressed together, soft and hard. She stumbles, her foot catching on a root, and I wrap one arm around her waist from behind, the other one a counterweight to balance us so we don't fall. The water pack that I'm wearing like armor forms a strange padding that hits her own water pack.

She squeals, and I look down. There's water on my leg.

"The mouthpiece. It backwashed," she says, giggling as we look down at the ground to find a small puddle, no bigger than a grapefruit, at the base of her foot.

I don't move away. My arm stays wrapped around her, the spare one sliding up and down her arm, stopping at the thin, fragile bones of her wrist.

"Duff," she whispers.

Sudden movement up ahead leads to leaves fluttering on our right as a gaggle of Boy Scouts run past us, one at a time, forcing us to move over to the left off the path. They're clearly in competition, the boy in front pelting at a crazy speed down a thirty-degree incline. Lily watches, laughing even harder. A beleaguered parent brings up the end of the pack. I count seven kids huffing. The mom looks at us and gives us an indulgent smile.

"If only we could bottle that energy," she says, pointing ahead, taking a swig out of a stainless-steel water bottle. "You going to the summit?" she asks, stopping, plainly looking for an excuse to take a break.

"Yes," Lily says.

"Not sure," I say at the same time, wanting to hedge my bets. Giving people as little information as possible is standard operating procedure for me. I can't break it, not even with Lily in my arms.

"Rain clouds are bad up there," the woman says, catching Lily's eyes. "Lots of us are leaving."

Lily just smiles back.

I could get used to this. I could get used to the feel of her skin beneath my fingertips. I could get used to the sound of her laughter as we walk outside, bathed in nature, with hours to do absolutely nothing. I could get used to breathing and having no meaning beyond existing with her. I could get used to the privilege of imagining a future. I could even get used to a world without vigilance.

The opposite of control is love. Lily is showing me that.

The Boy Scout leader passes us reluctantly, moving quickly, calling ahead to her charges to slow down, to wait, to be safe. Lily turns and wraps her arm around my waist, the gesture casual, but also questioning. I confirm what she's asking by doing the same, moving my arm up to her shoulders, the height difference from the incline making it more comfortable.

Letting her into my sphere of influence is one thing.

Letting her into my physical space for a purpose not solely connected to keeping her alive is another.

For the next two miles, according to my GPS, we just walk. Muscles have memory, but they also have flexibility. They move into the unknown, mapping the territory with oxygen, with reflex, with constant agility. Our proprioceptive sense of the world forces us to be like a gyroscope. We are aware of every part of our body as it exists on various planes, moving with a melodic grace that requires attention, but it's the absence of focus that allows the beauty to come in.

Bodies can do extraordinary things in that space of the unexpected.

But it's that empty space we create to allow for the unknown that Lily is carving out inside me.

It's entirely on me to let it happen.

"Left or right?" she calls back as we hit a fork in the path.

I shrug. "You're the one in charge. You pick."

She playfully hits my shoulder. "Duff! Come on. Don't make me decide everything."

"Burdened by choice," I joke, and peel us off to the right. The path is wider this way, and there is more light coming in from the treetops. At the end of a long, open section, the path narrows and moves up sharply. We bend forward at the hips as we climb up, feet setting carefully on solid rock after solid rock, climbing like we're walking on a ladder that has rungs on either side of a straight pole.

It's hard work, but it's good work, the kind that makes your muscles burn from achievement. Her bare calves are in front of my face, the muscles twitching and curving with exertion. Beauty is before my eyes, a restless but certain motion that is mesmerizing.

The sound of my breath in my ears develops a cadence, a uniform drumbeat that takes over. We climb, and we climb, and we *climb*, until the trees thin out and the path levels off. Lily can't go fast, but what she lacks in speed she makes up for in slow, steady forward motion.

Which is her character.

We stop. To the right is a steep cliff, thick rock jumbled with scrub. There are few trees down that side. It's glacier-like, as if someone stood in the sky and used an ax, chopping over and over again to create a divot hundreds of feet into the ground.

Lily stares out over the ledge. It's a good three hundred feet away, so plenty of safe space. "We are nothing, aren't we?" she says quietly. "It takes coming out here to realize it." A sad smile plays with her lips. "I nearly died two years ago because of some random event. Some random man shooting me. Wrong place, wrong time. An insignificant blip."

"Not just any man," I correct her. "Romeo." *And you're anything but insignificant*, I think.

"Yes, Romeo. But in a larger sense, a fellow being sent out to do something evil. They just picked the wrong person."

"It was an accident."

"It was an accident that I was shot, sure. But in some ways, it was an accident that I'm alive."

"It's a damn *miracle* you're alive," I choke out, hating her words.

Hating them because she's right.

"What if, Duff? What if you hadn't been there fast enough to stop the blood loss from the bullet? What if the doctors in the

ER hadn't done everything right? What if there hadn't been a benefactor like Jane to pay for everything you could possibly imagine? What if my mother hadn't been so aggressive about my care? What if Romeo had come to my room and decided to use a pillow to smother me? What if that spider that he planted had actually bitten me? What if—"

I silence her with a kiss. All the randomness, the feeling of being a speck of dust in the galaxy, of being unable to control destiny, fades with her in my arms. Her soft mouth moves against mine, warm, wet tongue so good, so right. As the sky darkens and wind begins to threaten a storm, I kiss her until she feels important. Significant.

Mine.

"This is going to end badly, isn't it?" she says against my mouth.

"What?"

She titters. "Not this. Not us. Whatever *us* is. I mean the whole situation with Romeo. He works for the *president*, for God's sake. It'll be my word against his."

"You're going to be open? Finally tell someone other than us?"

"I have to. I can't keep lying to Mom and Dad. To my family. It's exhausting."

"You're not afraid anymore?"

"Of course I'm afraid. I'm terrified. But now that you, Jane, Silas, and Drew know, the cat's out of the bag. Might as well tell the police."

"I think that's smart. Just not yet."

Her hand goes over my heart. Our eyes meet. Wind whips her hair in a horizontal line across her face, covering her nose.

"Lily, listen—there's something you need to know."

"There's a lot I need to know," she says, laughing.

"This is about the poisonous spider."

"What about it?"

"I found out some new information. These spiders were connected to El Brujo. The drug kingpin."

"What?"

167

"He owned enormous flower farms in Colombia. He used shipments to the U.S. to hide drugs. The spiders were in them. And a handful of spider deaths are loosely connected to him."

"How?"

"Looks like he, ah..." Damn. How do I tell her this?

"He what?"

"He put a few spiders in a cage with his victims and let the spiders bite them."

"WHAT? I thought he was the guy who cut women's arms and legs off for sick fun."

"That, too."

"How do you kill a spider when you don't have a foot to... oh." Stepping back, she moves out of our warm embrace.

Way to kill the mood.

"How do you know this?" she asks.

"I have sources."

"The darknet?"

"Something like that."

"You're being vague."

"Have to."

"You must hold a lot of really horrific information inside that head of yours." She stands on tiptoes and brushes her fingertips along my scalp.

I sigh. "More than you can imagine."

"You sound like you carry the weight of the world between your ears."

"Some days it feels like that."

"Feels? Are you going to talk about feelings, Duff? I thought you didn't have those."

"I do now."

This time, the kiss is raw, hard, unyielding, and Lily gives it right back.

A rumble of thunder in the distance makes us separate. She squints over the long horizon, eyes taking in the brewing storm.

Lily pulls out her phone. "Cliché, I know," she says with a self-deprecating tone. "But it's so beautiful."

So are you, I think but don't say.

Frowning, she makes a little sound at her phone. "Huh. No signal. We're really way out here, aren't we?"

I look around, pinpricks of unease making my hands twitch. My fingers curl into fists. "Yeah. We are. Where'd all the other people on the trail go?"

"Must have gone left when we went right." As she plays with her phone, I listen. Carefully.

Nothing out of the ordinary.

I still don't like it.

"We need to stick to the trail," I call out to her as she moves closer to the edge of the cliff. Although she's still at least two hundred feet from the edge, my nerves jangle, senses shifting into overdrive.

Something is *wrong*.

CHAPTER 26

*R*acing towards her, I act like a shield, but against what? It's like protecting her from the wind. The smoky clouds. The leaves that sway in the breeze. I can't keep Lily safe from a predator I can't see.

Even *I* don't have that kind of power.

"What is wrong?"

"I don't like this."

"Don't like nature?" Standing on tiptoe, she kisses my cheek. "Let's take a selfie," she whispers.

"What?"

"A selfie. You know. Where you point the camera towards yourself and–"

"I know what a selfie is. Why do you want one?"

"To have a picture of us together."

"There are plenty of those out there," I grunt.

"What? Where?" She brightens.

"In your file."

"My file? I have a–oh. Right." Her face darkens. "That's not the kind of photo I mean."

"There are plenty of them with us together," I say, my mind a database flipping through all of the video and surveillance-camera footage that makes up tens of thousands of gigs on a server somewhere. Every image is searchable. Every image is meticulously documented. We are being surveilled here, which means every time I touch her, I could be giving Romeo more leverage.

"Come here," she says, waving me closer. I put my head next to hers and scowl. "That's not a selfie, Duff," she chides.

I grin.

"Now you look like Pennywise the clown without makeup."

I grin wider.

"Duff!"

"What?" I say, eyes on the camera.

"I want a picture of us together."

"This *is* a picture of us together," I say through my smiling, closed teeth.

"A real one."

She sounds a little hurt, which makes me feel bad.

"Then you have to call me Sean. I only give real smiles when you use my real name."

She starts clicking photos just as I turn away, hearing the sounds of footsteps crunching on forest debris. Two people are moving across the path between the trees and the brush. To my relief, it's Ralph and Justin. But they're coming at us from the woods and not up from the trail. Maybe one of them had to take a leak. Maybe both.

My system stands down, the need for vigilance less. This is why we have backup.

"Hey," Ralph says, not smiling. "What's going on?"

"We're taking a selfie," Lily says, turning towards them. She holds the camera aloft. "You want to join us?"

For a split second, the two guys share a look. It's microscopic. Lily doesn't notice it. Lily's not *supposed* to notice it. The spot at the base of my neck tingles again. Every breath I take is slow and ponderous at the same time that blood rushes quickly to my hands, my feet, my lips, my cheeks.

We've been set up.

Holy shit.

"I thought you guys were behind us," I say, keeping my voice low. My hand moves up the side of my body, resting at my hip. I look like a guy who's taking a break. This is more than a chess game. If I'm wrong, then I'm just an over-reactive freak with a trigger-happy complex. If I'm right, no one's going to know about it because I'll be dead.

Lily notices the change in me, even if she's oblivious to the signals Ralph and Justin are putting out.

"We just thought we'd catch up to you." Justin gives Lily a dazzling smile. He's a charmer. Lots of guys in security are. If you're the type to sleep with women in order to get information out of them, you can go far in this field. Justin's one of those. He moves close to Lily, his gait one of practiced sensuality. "It's beautiful up here, isn't it?" he says.

I pay attention to the pattern of their body language. Both move behind us, separate from each other at opposite ends of an imaginary horseshoe that Lily and I are in the center of, with the open section facing towards the cliff.

"Did Gentian and Foster tell you to come here?" I ask. "To come here close to us? You have some message to deliver?"

Justin pulls his phone out of his front pants pocket and laughs. "No signal up here. Can't communicate with home base."

"Yeah, I noticed that, too," Lily says, completely oblivious. "My phone doesn't work, either."

"It's so remote up here," Ralph says. "It's just man vs. nature, isn't it?"

"You sound like English class," Lily says. "Man vs. Nature, Man vs. Man."

"Right. Man vs. Man," I say under my breath.

She stiffens. That was my goal. *Now* she gets it.

Instinct makes her move closer to me. I can see her pulse jump, a vein in her neck doing a dance of terror. No part of me thought I would be in this position today, but here I am. Calculations begin, a complex algorithm involving my gun, Lily, me, Justin, Ralph, and the chances of getting out of this alive.

I can't predict.

There's no probability formula that gives me odds that are even remotely testable. I do know this: I'm about to fight for Lily's life.

But if I don't save mine, too, she hasn't got a chance.

"We're good," I tell them. "You can resume your positions."

"New positions. Change of orders." The sky rumbles. Justin looks out at the clouds and grins. "Rain. Perfect."

Ralph catches his eye. I know what they're thinking.

Rain washes away evidence. My blood.

Lily's blood.

"Change of orders?" innocent Lily asks, breaking my train of thought.

Ralph grins.

Justin doesn't.

He's the one who makes the first move, the gun pointed at me. "We're doing this the easy way," he says as Lily gasps, the sound turning into a high shriek.

"What are you doing?" she shouts at him.

"Ask Duff." A self-satisfied huff accompanies the answer, his tongue rolling in his cheek as his face loses all expression.

Her questions buy me time, precious seconds I need to figure out what they're planning. If I were them, what would I do?

"Aren't you two cute?" Ralph says to her, moving closer. "Lovers on a hike. How sweet. Such a shame you were taking a selfie and didn't pay attention to the cliff." He snatches the phone out of Lily's hand and scrolls through the photos. Holding the screen up to Justin, he sneers. "Perfect. She just took one." He looks at me. "You definitely shouldn't look to the right when you smile, Duff. Your left side is your best."

"I'll keep that in mind next time I model for Victoria's Secret."

Lily gapes at me.

But Ralph's taunting makes me realize what they're doing. Gives me insight.

Gives me an opening.

They're on orders not to shoot. No one wants a bullet in our bodies. This is planned to look like an accident. They might have to pick us up and throw us off that cliff, but they aren't going to shoot us.

Which means there's a chance.

But hell if I know how to find it.

"Stateless, huh?" I blurt out to Ralph, who flinches. Cold, dead eyes meet mine as he recovers.

Hit a nerve.

Survival instinct kicks in. I've killed before. Plenty of times. In battle, or to defend myself or a client. Going into that head-space is like flipping off a long row of circuit breakers until all you're left with is night-vision goggles.

Except instead of lights, you shut off emotion.

You have to. Panic gets you killed. Emotions are great when your life isn't being threatened.

When you're about to be terminated by a predator, they're a liability.

Justin moves towards Lily, making me spread my arms, blocking him.

"It's two on two, Duff, and one of you isn't a challenge. We can do it easy or hard."

"Or not at all."

"Too late."

"Too late for you and Justin, you mean."

"Duff!" Lily wheezes, her voice gone, terror turning her vocal cords into a pressure cooker. "Help!"

I'm trying, I think as Ralph lunges, the two of them going after her. Double teaming makes sense. They know I'll fight them off, and right now, they risk falling off the ledge if they divide and conquer.

I go for my gun, but the damn water vest has shifted just enough during the hike to block the holster. As Ralph roughly pushes Lily, knocking into her knees and spilling her to the ground, Justin shoves his hands under her armpits hard enough for her to scream.

I pancake the pile of them.

My vest squirts water everywhere as I splay and flatten them, Lily making screamy-squeaky noises, the guys grunting and working to move and gain leverage. An elbow. A calf. Anything with thick hair gets my fingernails. I bite the thick flesh of Ralph's bicep, making him elbow me in the nose. Doesn't break it, but blinds me for a second. The vest presses against me until a muffled pop is followed by a rush of water that covers Justin's head.

But it lubricates us, too.

Thunder rolls in the distance, the air rich with misty rain-drops that aren't quite committing to the storm just yet.

But Ralph and Justin are committed.

Ralph sucker punches my kidneys, going hard.

"Knife!" Justin grunts as I stand, using my thighs as leverage. Lily scrambles up, cradling her left arm, pale as a ghost.

Ralph sweeps her off her feet and makes an awkward jog for the cliff, limping slightly.

"EYES!" I shout to her. She reaches up. Ralph pins her arms.

She head butts him, slightly off center, the bridge of her nose hitting his right eye socket.

And then I see white. Justin lands a right hook on my temple and I'm down, on my stomach, my ankles in his grip and my lips dragging on the dirt. Stones bounce against my teeth, my hip bones screaming as I twist, fingers turning bloody as I grab at anything, nothing, to prevent being thrown off that cliff.

The force of being dragged hikes up my deflated water vest, revealing my gun belt. I fumble. The holster itself snaps, gun spinning off like a child's toy top, until I hear it skitter, then bang as it falls over the cliff's edge and beta tests what's about to happen to me and Lily.

No.

NO!

Justin has to let go of my feet to get the right torque to shove me over. Tightening my core, I use my weight to roll over and up, on my feet within seconds. Our eyes meet as he reconfigures his plan, but I'm a split second ahead of him, charging mid-section, remembering tackle days in high school football.

I take him down, his nose making a satisfying crunch as we whack our heads on a flat rock embedded in the dirt.

"Aaaaaiiieeee!' Lily screams. I look to my left to find Ralph on her, pressing against her like he's raping her, using his feet to push both of them forward, her hair caught under her, pulling her chin up. Blood smears her forehead. I jump up before Justin can react, run over, and grab Ralph's hair, yanking him high.

And then I get both hands on his jaw. Closing my eyes, I feel for it, training flowing into my wrists like blood.

Snap.

His legs twitch, arms flailing, the fresh scent of bowels and piss filling my nose as I drop him, moving just enough to make sure he doesn't fall on Lily, who is flat on her back, fully clothed, staring up at me like I'm the monster.

And then I'm down, face in Ralph's dead hand, Justin pulling me by one leg as Lily screams, eyes fixed on Ralph.

"Lily! RUN!" I scream.

She's frozen.

"RRRRUUUUUUUNNNNNNNNN!" I shout again, knowing it's futile. Lily *can't* run. Justin's got a death grip on me. The sudden snap and crackle of lightning behind me is followed by all the hair on my arms and legs standing on end, ozone permeating the air.

By the time the rain begins, two of us will be dead.

Question is: Which two?

CHAPTER 27

Cold heat, paradoxical and searing, rips across the length of my thigh.

Justin's got a knife, one that slips out of his hand as I use my arms to lift my chest up hard and high, like an overdone push up, looking like a lethal breakdancer. I'm propelling my full body weight as high as I can to disorient and destabilize him.

It works.

Blood runs up to my hipbone as my heel catches his face, grazing enough to buy me time. He stumbles back, pinwheeling, until I turn around.

His face. His face says he knows.

Death finds a way to hat-tip itself. It always does.

But evil can snatch victory from the jaws of defeat, too.

My knee bends painfully as his hand catches my ankle, this time in desperation. My ass grinds into the ground as he slides over the edge of the cliff, road rash flaying me, my bleeding fingertips too weak to get purchase.

"DUFF!" Lily screams as Justin goes over, his shout vibrating up between my legs, over my gut, into my throat.

And then hands, one around my neck, one under my armpit.

"Let go," I try to say, but it's a gurgle. Lily's got me, barely, but she's choking me, the water vest under my neck, pressing on my carotid artery. I'll die this way. Between her attempt to keep me from plummeting, and Justin hanging on to me, I'm dead either way if this doesn't change–*fast*.

And more than four hundred pounds of muscle can't be held up by a woman who weighs less than half of me.

Kicking, I use my free leg to flail. Justin's fingers find my waistband and dig in. Bastard's turning me into a climbing wall at a city gym, fingers turning into crampons, my flesh just a surface he can use in pursuit of his goal.

To live.

My hands are free, but oxygen's sparse. I punch, hard, short jabs designed to make him twitch. Leverage is my friend here.

Until Lily moves.

Letting go of my neck, she puts all her strength into the arm that's under my pit, fingernails puncturing my skin. I inhale, until Justin headbutts me.

And then he recoils, sudden and powerfully, pulling me into thin air for a second as he pulls back, his grip lessening. A big, sharp rock the size of my fist falls between our bodies.

Again, it happens.

This time, a heavy rock bounces off his head and onto my chest, the impact making my lungs seize up. His eyes meet mine, face in a snarl, but the jagged line over his brow is unmistakable. Gritty and streaked with dirt, the line fills in with blood.

"LILY!" I scream as he turns to deadweight, dragging me down. Hands behind me, I find a thin root from some kind of bush. It's all I've got. Giving up my punching hand, I thread my way as deep as possible into the loose soil, praying.

Prayer is highly underrated as a tool in hand-to-hand combat.

His foot pulls up, ass punching out as he climbs me, my hipbone the equivalent of a rock ledge. My stomach twists and the air bleeds out of me in a hiss that feels like I'm being exorcised.

Another rock. Lily's elbow is at an odd angle to my right, the side she's holding up. My shoulder blades scream, threatening to separate, my head still above grade. I'm bent and bending further, about to snap.

I don't care.

As long as we don't drag Lily down with us, I'll have fulfilled my mission. She'll survive.

Even if I don't.

Pain turns into a buzzing nothingness in moments like this. Instinct is all that matters. My hold on the root is weakening, Justin crushing my liver with his hiking boot, my free arm punching his kidneys as hard as I can. His belly presses into my face, smothering me.

Can't breathe.

Can't yell.

Can't do anything but hold on.

He goes slack, the sudden dead weight making me lose my grip as his jacked-up leg loosens, going straight, taking the skin on my hips with him. Sliding down a foot or so, his face meets mine.

His knife sticks out of the top of his head, the handle crooked. Lily speared him like a cocktail olive on a toothpick.

The buzzing in my ears stops.

And then I hear Lily's screams.

"HELP!" she's screaming. I want to tell her to stop, to shut up, to RUN, to live, but I can't.

I can't, because Justin tips back, his fingers still deep in my waistband, his body falling away from mine like peeling contact paper off its backing, our bodies meeting like a Y.

Except his hand is so deep in my damned pants, he's about to take me down.

Gurgling and twitching, he's flopping away. Lily's second hand goes under my other arm, securing me as I grab the knife handle and yank, hard. I toss the knife backwards, where I hear it skitter away from Lily. We might need it, in case more are coming for us.

My spare hand slides between Justin's belly and mine and wrenches his hand out, the crack of his bones not sickening.

It's blissful.

It's the sound of freedom.

I hike up my knees and shove, hard, until he's BASE jumping, upside down, back to the wind.

Except this isn't a pleasure sport.

My kick is too hard, though, bringing Lily forward, her center of gravity off balance.

"DUFF!" she screams.

"Stop moving."

"I can't! My heels, they're sliding."

"Lily, let go of my right side."

"WHAT? No! You'll fall! You'll fall like, like him—"

"Trust me. Let go. Only one side. Don't grab my neck."

"But—"

"NOW!"

She obeys, but doubles down on her hold on my left.

Pivoting off the thin root's marginal help, I get my heels into the hillside and push up an inch or two, just enough to use my core. Something in my spine pops, my shoulder screaming, the back of my head feeling like a rolling pin is being pressed into it.

Her hands get under the vest and pull hard.

And I'm up.

Mission accomplished. Lily's alive.

I'm just a bonus.

CHAPTER 28

*T*wo hundred pounds of dead meat is still one tenth of a ton.

I grab Ralph under the arms and make a split-second decision as the thunder gets closer, roiling rain clouds suddenly turning into my savior. Dragging his crooked body takes all the leg strength I've got, glutes working overtime.

"What are you doing?" Lily calls out.

I stop short of the edge of the ledge, change position, and get down in a lunge, heels of my palms on Ralph's thigh and ribs. Blood that poured freely minutes ago starts to congeal, the skin of his face taking on a sickly yellowish pallor.

"WHAT ARE YOU DOING?" Lily screams as gravity kicks in, the tipping point taking hold, Ralph's body sliding along the dry ground. Moving slowly, I work to make sure I don't get pulled down with him.

"Shhhh."

"You're throwing him off the cliff?"

"That's what–" *grunt* "–they were going to do to you. To me." Ralph's not bleeding anymore. Corpses don't have a pulse, so they don't pump blood, but they do leave a mess.

The sound of his body tumbling down the ravine is like putting three grapefruit in a dryer on high.

The crunch of bone against rock makes me turn away swiftly. No one needs to watch that.

Not even the guy who'll have to give a detailed report to Drew Foster.

"Did you just–" Lily's voice descends into mewling sounds, choked outrage turning her nonverbal.

A raindrop on the back of my neck makes me skitter, falling on my ass. Adrenaline makes our bodies react in weird, impulsive ways. Fear spikes my heart rate. I start to hyperventilate.

Training brings me back under control in seconds.

"B-b-but they're already dead!" Shaking hard, Lily's teeth chatter. Oh, no.

Shock could render her completely immobile. We need to be swift and flexible now if we're going to get away from this before the authorities figure it out.

I need Drew and Silas to help hide this mess.

"We need to make them disappear. Remove the evidence," I tell her as Mother Nature cooperates. Nothing like a rainstorm to aid and abet.

"You can't just make a person disappear!"

"They did it to my brother," I spit out before I realize what I'm saying.

Remember? Adrenaline makes our bodies do weird shit.

Our mouths, too.

"Your brother? Someone killed your brother?"

"No. Not dead."

"Sean, you're jabbering nonsense! We need to call the police!"

"NO!" I bellow, losing control. My shout echoes, hard, fierce, firm.

She recoils.

"You–you killed them! WE killed them. BOTH OF THEM!" she screams, scrubbing her face with her hands, smearing blood everywhere. It's in her hair, on her eyelids, all along the edges of her lips, which she licks.

And then she starts to gag.

"Lily, I–"

"NO!" she screams, spitting, stepping backwards. Backing

away from me, she looks wild, like a teen girl in a horror movie, the butt of a cruel joke. "My *God*, Sean," she says in a hiss-shriek that is worse than any shout. "You killed him with your bare hands. You snapped his neck like a... you know..." She frowns, freaked out. "Turkey. Neck. Bone."

"Wishbone," I fill in, dread seeping into my bones. She's forgetting words. The stress could set off a vascular event.

"You–you–"

Plus, she's using my real name.

"Lily, come closer to me." If she panics, she'll walk herself right off the ledge.

"And I–I shoved a knife into a man's head! I–the pain, oh, the pain in my arm as the bone, his skull, I–"

"Lily, come here."

"Why?" I can taste her hysteria. "*Why?*"

"Because I want you to be safe."

"We just killed two men! You broke that guy's neck like you were opening a water bottle. Just a twist! How can *you* be safe?"

"I killed them to save you. To save me."

"You killed them for me."

"Yes."

"And now they're dead."

"Yes."

"They're dead because of me."

"No. They're dead because they tried to kill us."

"Both of us?"

"Yes."

"Why would someone want to kill you, Sean?"

"Plenty of reasons."

"Why me?" she begs. Her voice is so sorrowful, it makes my mind go blank. I can't afford to let that happen.

"Lily. We have to get this place cleaned up."

"Clean?" Holding up her hands, she stares at them. Rusty blood covers her fingernails. When our eyes meet again, the whites of her eyeballs fairly glow.

"Yes, clean."

"But they're dead."

"Yes."

"You killed them."

Oh, shit.

The circularity of her words is a result of shock. Shaking, she runs her bloodied hands up and down her arms. Gooseflesh ripples across her exposed skin. As she breathes in jerky, gasping breaths, I assess the situation. There isn't too much blood. Most of it's from Ralph's broken nose and Justin's head wound. Lily has surface scrapes from fighting with Ralph and Justin, but nothing more. Her legs look fine. Eyes, too.

She's capable of walking.

Can she run? No. I know she can't. Not yet.

But first, I need to make sure she gets away from that ledge.

"Lily," I say in a soothing voice, my calm tone rising above the rush of my own pulse in my ears. "Please come closer to me."

"No." As she looks down over the cliff at Justin and Ralph's bodies, a low moan starts in the back of her throat.

"Lily. Please," I say, going as emotional as I can. I need to enact a rescue plan. Lily falling off the ledge is not part of my plan.

"No."

"Then sit down."

"What?"

"SIT!" I say through gritted teeth, my tongue lifted in my mouth, the word guttural and strong.

She stays standing. "No. If I sit, you could hurt me."

"I'm not going to hurt you."

She looks down again at the dead bodies.

"Lily, if I wanted to hurt you, I'd have done it a long time ago."

"They–he–he picked me up. He was choking me. His arm cut off my air and my skin pounded so hard, it felt like I was going to burst and he–"

Wild eyes meet mine. They're ringed with red dots, broken blood vessels from being strangled. The spots look like freckles that cheated death.

"Lily." I wave my fingers towards me, like guiding someone

through parallel parking, except the stakes are so much higher here. "Come away from the ledge." Calculations kick in as I take in her location, her weight, momentum if I have to run and grab her, and whether I can move fast enough to overcome her panic and not roll us both off that ledge.

"You–you killed them." She takes a step back.

"I did." I step forward.

"Why?" *Step.*

"Because you are too important to let them kill you." *Step.*

"I don't–I can't–I just wanted a hike!" *Step.*

She's about four steps away from falling off.

Three.

"Lily!"

Two.

I have no choice.

I charge.

CHAPTER 29

I drop to the ground and scoop my legs behind her, one going high enough to make sure I don't accidentally kick her off the damned ledge myself. Laws of physics work with me, for once, and she comes crashing forward, crying out as she falls on my torso.

I roll on top of her, pinning her in place.

"Don't move. You almost fell."

"Don't hurt me!"

"I'm trying to save you, Lily."

"Get off me!"

"No."

Rain pounds on my back as she goes still under me, body tense.

"I'm not trying to hurt you, Lily. I'm trying to save you."

"You did. You saved me." A thousand-mile stare meets my gaze when we look at each other.

Shock.

I move off her, slowly, keeping my knees on either side. Water smashes against my back in icy spikes as the wind whips the storm closer to us, the air cooling second by second.

"You saved me, too."

At my words, her face screws up in pain, the horror of what's

186

just happened pouring out of her expression. People don't let you see the reality of what goes on inside.

I'm witnessing it now.

Trauma does that.

"Lily," I say, bending over, stroking her wet cheek with the back of my bloodied hand. "We have to go. Now."

"I don't think I can walk."

"I'll help you. We need to get in cell range. Need to call Silas and Drew now. We don't know who else is coming."

"Who else? I'm pretty sure they closed the–" Angry eyes meet mine. "Dirt. Wide. Walk on it."

"Trail."

"Yes! They closed the trail."

"There may be more than Ralph and Justin coming."

Her mouth drops open in an O of horror. I offer my hand, pink water dripping onto her stomach in a stream.

Lily shakes her head violently, like a wet dog. Then she stands.

Then she limps, my arm about to go around her waist. She shakes me off, palm flat on my soaked chest, my water vest ripped and flap hanging open.

"I got it," she says, starting to unclip her own vest.

"Don't," I say, looking around the site for evidence. "We don't want to leave anything behind."

"Then get the knife," she says, squinting beyond me.

That she would remember is a sign. A sign of a survivor. There's a stone-cold chamber inside this woman, where reason and forethought live. She's clicked into that place.

What I saw earlier was sheer panic.

What I'm seeing now is cold. Calculated.

And it explains so much about her.

I find the shining metal, wet but clean now, resting against a rock that juts out from the ground by the trail. Oddly enough, Justin's gun is next to it. Folding the knife, I shove it in my pocket. The gun I stick in my belt, safety on.

Lily's phone is about ten feet away, glass shattered. Lily approaches me, limping, holding her left elbow. Seeing the phone before I can retrieve it, she bends down, using her bad arm.

"At least *I* didn't break it this time," she says somberly.

"Jesus," I say under my breath, a rare splash of emotion bubbling up to the surface. I don't do this in crisis. Ever.

I guess I do when I'm with her.

"Nothing else is here," she says in a matter-of-fact voice. "Blood's being washed off the cliff already by the rain. We're good."

We're good.

The walk down the trail is quiet. Too quiet, at least between us. My head is pounding and I loop through the events, over and over, to make sure I understand the framework in which I have to perform.

JUSTIN AND RALPH *were ordered to kill us.*

They were supposed to make it look like we fell off the cliff.

They weren't allowed to leave a bullet wound in our bodies.

They sure as hell didn't expect to die.

HOW DO I know that last one?

Because so far, no one's on their heels.

Mud covers the trail, the flat parts enormous puddles. Trudging through, the water doesn't faze Lily, whose shoes are soaked as we walk through ankle-deep pools. She's got the thousand-mile stare that tells me we'll make it to the car.

Bzzz.

Our phones go off at the same time.

Signal kicked in.

I grab mine and immediately call Silas, who picks up on the first ring. Lily's trying to get her broken glass screen to work, but the phone rings until it just stops.

"Compromised," I snap into my phone.

"*What*? Who?"

"Ralph and Justin."

"Where are they?"

"Dead."

"I didn't say how, I asked where."

"At the bottom of a cliff."

"Lily?"

"Alive. Here. Headed to the car. Who else is coming after us, Gentian?"

"No one. Trust me."

I snort.

"Ralph and Justin? What do they have in common?" he asks.

"You tell me."

"This is a secured line. What happened?"

"Lily and I were hiking. They appeared. Took her phone. Used a gun to threaten but not shoot. Said it would look like a lovers' hiking mistake."

A line of expletives greets me. "Foster just stepped outside with a new client. I need to get him in here." I hear a chair scraping, a door opening, footsteps.

"How do you know he isn't in on this?"

"Drew and I are safe."

"Someone trying to kill me would say that, too. Ralph and Justin were in on something. Together."

"They have nothing in common. Never worked together before."

"They're dead in a ravine together forever, Gentian."

"You killed them both?"

"Yes." It's easier this way. Lily doesn't need the paperwork. The guilt is bad enough.

"Good work."

"You have no idea."

"Hold on."

We're good.

Lily's words tumble through my mind like a gemstone being polished by a jeweler as I listen to Silas's muffled voice briefing Drew.

"I'm getting a team on the way."

"Don't need to be attacked by my own guys again, Gentian."

"This one's cleared."

"So were Ralph and Justin."

Silence.

"Say it, Gentian."

"There's one thing they have in common. Hold on–Drew's saying something–he says..."

"Says what?"

"They're both stateless."

"So's Romeo."

Silence again.

I let out a low whistle that turns to a burble as rainwater slips over my lips. Lily gives me a funny look. I'm practically spitting.

That's the connection? Now we're suspicious of all the stateless guys? No way." My words catch in my throat as I slip on wet ground, inner thighs screaming as I regain control. My personal mission has always been to get closer to the stateless guys. To understand them.

To know how they work.

And maybe–just maybe–to find Wyatt.

"Not all of them, no," he replies. "But for now, with Lily–yes."

"Smart," I bark into the phone, the wind pushing hard at our backs. "Who's coming?"

"Drew and me."

"Both of you?"

"This is bad, Duff. We're on our way. We were at a meeting about half an hour from there. How long will it take you to get down?"

I look at Lily's body, which is curling in on itself. The walk down is going to be slow.

"About that."

Line goes dead.

Lily doesn't ask. Doesn't even look at me. She's in her own head space and as long as her legs work, we can get to the car faster than if I have to carry her.

Fast is good.

Fast is critical.

But slow and steady is better than nothing.

For twenty-five minutes, I find myself in a meditative state and in a vigilant framework at the same time. We can hold two different realities at the same time. Don't *like* to, but we can. Aside from a few woodland creatures who make me pivot and react too quickly, we're left alone for the rest of the hike.

The roof of the ranger hut is in the distance now as I look ahead, squinting to see through the thick rain. Tree cover makes the rain pound us less, the uneven drip from the leaves less than the sum total of the storm's full wrath. As the trail widens and branches off, I know the parking lot is close.

Drew and Silas appear as we make a turn, a thick tree obscuring them until there they are, a wall of suit, black umbrellas almost laughable, given how soaked we are.

They look like they're at a funeral.

Which is apt after what just happened.

Wordlessly, they usher us into their SUV, Silas at the wheel. Drew takes the car I drove, his spare keys in hand already. Ralph and Justin's car sits in its spot, a sickening reminder that they're broken and cracked on the rocks up there. Someone from Drew's company will take care of the vehicle.

I already took care of *them*.

As we pull out of the lot, Drew follows closely. We're a caravan. None of us will breathe easy until we're in a safe house.

The question is: is any house safe?

In the back seat, there are lined mylar blankets, disaster-wear designed to keep you warm even when you're wet. I pull one out and wrap Lily in it. She's stunned, silent, staring at the headrest in front of her. A puppet I move at will, until her chill sharpens and she shakes.

Good.

That means her circulation works.

We'll deal with the trauma it indicates later.

I perform the same ritual on myself, knowing I need medical attention, the long gash up my thigh stinging like hell. Inside the cocoon of the mylar blanket, I touch it with raw fingers. A wide cut. Not to the bone. And the bleeding's stopped.

"Duff?" Silas calls back. "Need a doctor?"

"Nah. Just a flesh wound."

He barks out a sound that isn't even close to a laugh. "Don't want you bleeding out."

I hold up my hands. He looks in the rearview mirror and just shakes his head.

"If I'm bleeding out, it's through my fingertips."

"You need to clean that shit. Antibiotics."

"Right. Got a kit back home."

"That where you want to go? Your place?"

"Think it's safe enough?"

"I think the ranch is safest."

I look at Lily.

"I don't think she can handle a plane ride, Silas."

Lily sniffs, wipes the end of her nose, and leans on my shoulder, curling up against me. The pressure of her body against mine makes it easier to take a good, long, deep breath. My diaphragm has been damn near between my ears. Shallow breaths come with stress.

"A breach like this is huge, Duff. Drew's beside himself."

"Bet he is."

My words make Silas's eyes narrow in the mirror.

Lily's phone buzzes in her pocket. She looks but doesn't respond. Can't. It's too broken. Maybe she is, too.

"You should talk to your mom and dad," I whisper.

"How did you know it's them?" she asks slowly, sleepily, burrowing into me like she can hide from the world if she gets in close enough. I wish that were true. She yawns, her hot breath warming my ribs.

"Lucky guess. Let them know you're okay."

"How can I do that?"

"Are you?"

"No."

CHAPTER 30

"*I* don't like this," Drew growls, prowling outside the car. We're in the parking garage of my building.

"It's the best alternative," Silas argues. "Patch Duff up, give us time to think, give Lily a break. She's a TBI patient, Drew. She could stroke out."

"That's a risk?" he asks, pinching the bridge of his nose.

I nod and sigh. "Yes. Doctors keep telling her she needs to reduce stress."

"Good luck with that."

"No shit."

"If flying's too much, our choices are limited," Silas interjects. "We've got a few places here, but–"

"And my place is one of them. Limited entrances and exits. Few windows. Tiny. Easy to protect," I interject.

Silas gives Drew a look I could never get away with.

Drew sighs. "It's our best option out of a pile of shit options."

"We'll all need a long shower after this."

"Speaking of showers," Silas says, giving me a long look up my body, "and speaking of shit, you look like a six-foot tower of it. That's a nasty cut on your leg. Knife?"

"Yup."

"You need stitches."

"I need a shower, some antibiotic cream, and Krazy Glue."

"You need a shrink," Drew says.

"Don't we all?"

The one and only laugh between us pours out.

Lily chooses this exact moment to pop open her car door and step out. Glaring at three guys chuckling after the horror of the day, she asks, "Where are we going?"

"My place."

Her eyes dart to me, widening suddenly. "Your face!"

"What about it?"

"Scratches. You have–" Looking down, she sees my leg. "Oh my God! You need stitches!"

Drew clears his throat. "Nah. Duff'll just lick it clean and close it up with some Play-Doh and masking tape."

Indignation blasts out of her, all of it pointed at Drew.

"Are you INSANE?" she screams.

"See?" I nudge him. "I do need a shrink."

Swallowing hard, he composes himself and gives Lily his full attention, looking behind her, clearing the area. "We need to get you upstairs to Duff's place. We're securing the area. We've got a team here."

"A team? Like Ralph and Justin?" Her voice is ice.

"That mistake won't happen again."

"How do you know?"

"We're–"

Drew looks at his phone as a text buzzes in, eyebrows turning down hard. "What the–*no*." His eyes widen, jaw clenching.

"What's wrong?" Silas asks.

"I've gotta go. God damn it. Baby's sick. Sick enough for Lindsay to rush to the ER." A wild look I've never seen in him flares to the surface.

Fear.

"I didn't know she was sick."

"She wasn't. Runny nose this morning, now suddenly her ribcage is contracting when she breathes. Fingertips blue." His terse reply makes my stomach drop.

"Go. Your wife and kid are more important. We've got plenty of guys who can do this."

Don't need to tell Drew Foster twice. He nods sharply, an acknowledgment that is as close to emotion as I'm getting out of him.

"Gentian, take over."

"Of course."

"Don't say anything to the guys. We just need to reassign so there are no stateless here. But we can't tip anyone off that we're onto them."

"Got it, but that puts Lily at risk."

"There's no good way to do this, Duff."

"You think I don't know that?" Drew says, hands on hips.

"I hope the baby's okay. Lindsay, too," Lily says in a soft, small voice, eyes filling with tears.

The words are a gut punch to Drew, who closes his eyes and nods. "Thanks. Bye."

Storming off, he rounds a corner where I know the team's car must be.

"Let's get upstairs," I say, moving my sore bones as fast as I can, ignoring the pain. Silas gives a curt nod as two guys, Leroy and Joseph, appear from the same direction Drew just disappeared in. Leroy's huge, with a shaved head and the air of a man who's done time.

Joseph has a high voice, a thinning pate, and a perpetually pissed-off expression that is perfect for an ex-Secret Service agent. "Ready?" he asks.

Lily looks at me.

"Let's go."

Two minutes later, we're done with the stairs to my fourth-floor apartment. Lily needs help on the last flight. I'm worried. She's limping badly, holding her neck at a funny angle. The thousand-mile stare has turned worse; she's reflecting on the past.

Almost coma-like.

I can't lose her. She's alive, sure.

But you can be alive and hollow.

Trust me. I know.

Because she knows the layout of my place, her immediate beeline for the bathroom makes sense. Then the shower starts.

"Here," Leroy says, tossing a lightweight gym bag at me. I catch it. I knock softly on the bathroom door.

Nothing.

I press my ear to the wood.

Sobbing.

"Lily?" I say into the crack. "I've got clean clothes for you."

"Okay."

"Can I come in?"

"Sure."

Opening the door, I am greeted by the sight of her sitting on the toilet lid, head in her hands, the backs of them bruised and scraped up. She's openly crying, shoulders rising and falling with sobs. Steam fills the bathroom, the glass shower a triangle in the tiny space.

I bend, the long knife wound tearing as I do.

"I am so sorry," I say, the words ridiculous. We're trained never to say that to another operative in the field, because it's a useless, meaningless phrase.

It's the kind of bullshit you say when you have no power.

"I can't believe I killed someone."

"You did it to save me."

"And you killed someone to save *me*."

"We're even, then."

"I didn't know there was a scorecard."

"There isn't."

I want to touch her. My hand moves to her knee. She winces. I pull it back.

"I don't want to hurt you."

"You didn't. I'm—ouch, Duff. Your fingers. That's what I'm reacting to."

"It's nothing."

"It's horrifying."

"Worth it. I'd do it all over again, Lily, because you're alive."

This time, I put my hand on her shoulder and just leave it there. My palm buzzes along with my brain.

But she doesn't flinch.

And our eyes meet, hers red-rimmed and raw.

When she moves towards me, I'm surprised, arms around my neck clinging like she's about to fall and I'm her only hope. White mist in the room makes her ethereal, like a fairy queen out of battle, weary but pure.

My fingers hurt like a sonofabitch but that's okay.

Means I'm alive, too.

Stroking her back, I murmur sounds that don't make sense, talking to some piece of both of us we left behind a long time ago. She stands and begins to undress in front of me, open and unashamed.

"I need to be clean," she whispers. Sad eyes meet mine. "Will you shower with me?"

"Of course."

"I don't want to be alone."

"Right here with you, babe."

She begins to disrobe, her eyes cast down, until she looks up suddenly, catching her face in the mirror. Unblinking, she gawks at her reflection.

"We'll look better after a shower."

Shaking fingers reach up to touch her scar. "Nothing will make this better. Not water, not soap, not a loofah, not even a sand blaster. I haven't–oh, Duff. I didn't realize how bad it looks."

I walk behind her, hands on her shoulders, looking into the mirror, our dirty, blood-smeared faces staring back at us like a chronicle of the last few hours. Seared into my mind's eye, the image will never leave me. Not until the day I die.

Heedless of the mess, I press my lips to the back of her ear, kissing the scar. She cringes.

"It's beautiful. You're beautiful. Don't do this to yourself, Lily. Don't. Deflecting what you're feeling about the day doesn't mean you get to tear yourself down."

She doesn't answer. She just finishes getting out of her clothes, turning her gaze away.

Naked, filthy, bleeding, and as exposed—inside and out—as you can get, we squeeze into the small triangle of a shower, the room smelling like lemon, the shampoo stinging as it washes over my skin. Slick and slippery, so close to each other, I find myself acutely aware of every square inch. Not just her body. Not just mine.

Every space between. Outside the shower. In my apartment.

Space itself.

Lily turns around, her hands scraped up as she reaches for soap. Extending my arm above her, I take the bar and lather it, washing her back with big, long circles.

"If I could roll back time and stop them, I would," I say, the steam cushioning my words.

"I know."

"I'm so sorry." The words aren't enough.

"I–I can't stop thinking about his head. His skull. How the bone–how it hurt to hit him so hard. How my elbow screamed, like I was the one being, you know–" Her hands go up, gesturing. "Knife. Hit. Cut."

"Stabbed?"

"Yes!"

"No one imagines that until their first time," I say, commiserating. Losing her words shows she's still at risk, stress on display.

She shivers as if a ghoul walked over her grave.

"Sean, I don't think I can–" Her hips move away from mine, pivoting so we're not aligned, the temptation to move against her body in upward strokes removed entirely.

"*Shhhh.*" My fingertips cover her lips. "I don't want that. I just want to be with you. I want to help you wash away what happened today."

"It feels like it'll always be on my skin."

"I know. It always does. But it fades."

"Does it ever go away completely?"

"No."

198

"You never lie to me, do you?"

"Not when I can help it."

"You're not lying now, are you?"

"I wish I were, Lily. I wish I were." An ache no one can take away vibrates between us, her arms folding around my ribs, my chin resting on the top of her head, right where she stabbed Justin. We stand in the hot shower so long, it turns lukewarm, heat wasted, but then entropy reminding me it's not.

Nothing is wasted.

We finish rinsing, the shower over. There's a shift in consciousness that comes right after you kill someone. The horror is still there, relived over and over. Center stage, though, is a place for rotation when it comes to the mind. Nothing engages it for very long. Violence tends to stick the longest.

Violence and pain.

But at some point, it moves on to the next act. Never let it be said that the mind isn't fickle.

As we dry off, I pat her back gently with the towel. Bruises are appearing, silent reminders of today's violence that I'm glad she can't see. We dress. Leading her to bed, I close the bedroom door and turn down the covers. Lily crawls in, settling into place on the right. Curling my body around her, shielding her as best as I can, I hold her as she cries, great wracking sobs lifting her body off the mattress.

Slowly, slowly, they subside, like the tide changing with every wave.

And then the last sob. The last shudder. The last tear.

Lily fades off into sleep in my arms, safe.

Always safe in my arms.

CHAPTER 31

*S*leep eludes me. I'm half in, half out, hovering in that non-sleep state where we fool ourselves into thinking we're right on the brink of release. Clock says I've been in bed with her for three hours.

Feels like three days.

Like three seconds.

Eyes wide open, I look at the ceiling, the globe from the light fixture a weak spot. The window, too. Every point of entry comes to my attention, calling my name, taunting me.

Romeo and his stateless people have found the cracks and crevices no one else can.

I turn over on my belly and look at Lily. Her face is relaxed, her breathing even, a strand of hair across her nose. Like this, she's so innocent. So lovely.

But back on that hiking trail, she was so damn fierce.

Protecting her is no longer just a mission. Hasn't been for a long time. This is about protecting my heart, too.

Protecting it from being broken if they get to her.

Sliding out from under the covers carefully, I try not to wake her. She stirs. I freeze.

A long sigh comes out of her as she curls into a ball like a kitten.

Then peace.

My kitchen is empty. The guys are outside, I know, hidden so they're not obvious, but close enough in case of a crisis. I look in my fridge. Milk.

My stomach growls. Haven't eaten since this morning.

Look in the cabinet. A tin of chocolate-milk mix.

Two minutes later, I'm stirring mindlessly when cold dread fills me.

"Why are you up?"

I jump a thousand miles into the sky. "Bloody hell, Lily! Don't do that!"

"Do what?"

"Scare the shit out of me like that!"

"You sounded Irish when you said that."

"I fecking well have the right to," I reply, laying the accent on thick.

She laughs. It's good to hear that sound.

"Want some?" I offer up the glass. "Chocolate milk."

"You drink chocolate milk?"

"Sure."

"That's a kid's drink."

I shrug. "I was a kid once."

"It's hard to imagine that." She leans her ass against the edge of the counter, crossing her arms over her t-shirt. "What were you like as a kid? I saw that picture of you with your brother. The one Jane found."

"I was a kid. Like any other kid." I chug my milk. It suddenly doesn't taste good, but I drink it anyway.

"What really happened?" she whispers. "With your parents? Your brother?"

I'm down to the end, the gritty mix that sank to the bottom of my glass tasting like sweet dirt. I choke it down. I look around.

"I told you. They died. My brother disappeared."

"You can tell me the truth."

"I know."

"No, Sean," she says, stepping into my space, giving me her warmth. "Please tell me. *Please*. I need to understand you."

201

"I'm a simple guy."

"You're lying."

I grab the milk and the mix. Bending down, I find a bullet blender.

"What are you doing? I don't drink cow's milk. You know that."

"I want another one," I lie. The motor makes a steady, loud sound. Loud enough to screw with any listening devices in here. Pulling Lily close, I get my lips to her ear and say:

"It's simple. I want to find him."

"Find your brother? Wyatt?" She follows my lead and gets her mouth close to my ear. We flip-flop turns.

"Yes."

"How old is he again?"

"Twenty-seven."

"How old was he when he disappeared?"

"Four."

Her hand moves to her throat, a gesture of emotion. "Four? He was so little. I thought he was an adult, working for some secret agency."

"You're... close."

"Just say it, Duff. I don't have the energy to figure this out."

"He might work for the same people Romeo works for."

She turns red. "WHAT?"

"*Shhhhh*. He was stolen, Lily."

"Stolen? You mean kidnapped?"

"He was stateless."

"How? Are you–are *you*–?"

"No. I have a birth certificate. I'm not one of them."

"Then what–"

"I don't have much time. Can't blend forever."

She nods.

"My dad and mom were off-the-grid folks. Back to the land. Dad got weirder and more paranoid, my Gran said. By the time they had Wyatt, they decided not to record the birth. One day, when I was eleven and Wyatt was four, these men came. They beat my dad to death, shot my mom, made it look like a murder-suicide, and stole Wyatt."

"But you're alive!"

"They left me for dead."

She touches my scar. "Is that where you really got this? It wasn't from combat?"

I nod. I don't need to explain that an IED added to it years later.

"Gran went to Alice to find Wyatt. The local police were useless. Said there was no proof he ever existed, so... Gran took me home to Philly. Raised me best she could."

I turn off the blender.

I take a sip.

She just blinks and blinks and *blinks*.

Then her fierce hug bowls me over.

"You worked for her all those years because you're trying to find your brother?" she whispers, so soft, it might be the snore of a butterfly.

I nod.

"I can't believe I ever doubted you," she says, louder.

I yawn, and my jaw pops. It's contagious.

Hers does, too.

"C'mon," I tell her, offering my hand. "Let's go back to sleep."

"You think I'm going to sleep more after everything that's happened?"

"Then let's pretend to sleep."

We crawl into bed. She wiggles her ass against my front, inviting me to spoon. I do. It feels nice.

Better than nice.

Meanwhile, earthquakes happen inside me, tectonic plates rearranging themselves. No way am I sleeping tonight, but as that thought hits me, I yawn again.

Huh.

Maybe I'm wrong.

"Duff?" Lily asks in a sleepy voice.

"Yeah?"

"You need to buy almond milk for me."

"I will. Tomorrow."

"Good. Get a half gallon."

"That's a lot." An unfamiliar warmth washes over me, muscles feeling heavy and slow. She moves against me, seeking more skin contact. The comfort is nice. Relaxing.

Strange, yet familiar.

"I'm planning to be around for a while."

I squeeze her. "I'll get a gallon."

CHAPTER 32

*O*n my stomach. Sheet in my mouth. Blinking hard. No sunlight on my face. Sheers are pulled closed. I stare at the window.

Bang bang bang!

Someone's pounding on my door.

"Duff!" A muffled shout from the hallway. What's going on?

I sit up.

Except... I can't move. My hands are clenching the cotton sheets, fingertips like aging raw meat. I'm half naked, boxer briefs on, shirt off.

Lily.

Where's Lily?

There's three notes, pieces of paper torn out of a larger page. Three? Why three?

I squint. The notes become one. Not three. My eyes made three out of just one.

I lick my lips.

But my tongue can't move.

The president wants to see me.

. . .

THE PAPER FLUTTERS as I move my fingers to grasp it better, eyes focusing to read. That's Lily's handwriting, loopy and feminine. Even the i has a heart over it for the dot.

A thin tickle on the back of my hand makes me rotate my wrist.

I freeze.

Three black spiders stare back at me.

I focus.

No. Just one.

God, no.

"Lily," I whisper as I hold my hand up high, shaking the eight-legged black weapon off my middle finger, reaching for my gun. I grab it, the cold metal stabilizing me. My legs are rubber bands. I flop to the ground, willing my hips to work, my head pounding like someone's pressing a concrete block on it.

Standing on legs that shake like a broken compressor, I find the spider. An empty water glass from my bedside table makes a fine prison for it. This one needs to be kept whole.

BANG BANG BANG!

My front door flies open, the handle smashing a hole into the wallboard.

"DUFF!"

I look down at the spider inside the glass. The spider tries to find an out, scrambling, moving fast from side to side, wasting effort that is futile. As I try to watch it, the room spins.

Where is Lily?

Silas charges into the room as I drop back to the floor, knees weak, gun positioned down.

"What is wrong with you?" he asks, grabbing my jaw with one hand, yanking it up. He kicks the gun away. Shadows fill the doorway, two guys in suits.

I want to answer.

But I don't know.

I don't know what's wrong with me.

"Your eyes. They're like black pennies. What the hell are you on, Duff? You're an *addict?*" Contempt spits out of him with that last word.

"No," I say, my tongue coated with fur. "No."

Spider bites connected to El Brujo. Victims tortured by them. Lily's hospital room. The stateless turning against us. Romeo is stateless.

The president wants to see me.

"Where the hell is Lily?" Silas demands. "What did you do with her?"

I look at him, skin tingling, eyes rolling in different directions. I can't form the words. Can't think the thoughts. I'm spiraling down, down, down a drain like something you wash away into the sea.

He snatches the note. Reads it. Looks at me.

"Damn it," he hisses.

"Drug," I say. "Nee elp." The connection between my brain and my mouth isn't working. Is this what Lily felt like all those months?

"Knee help?"

"Elp me. Some-un drug... me. Lily. Elp Lily."

"Oh, shit," he says, moving with lightning speed between the guys hovering, barking orders into his phone as I fall on my back, staring up at the ceiling, the same glass globe that was the focus of my insomnia now the object of my doom.

It's been under my nose the whole time.

How could we all have *missed* it?

What if Monica Bosworth was never the mastermind? Not even El Brujo or Nolan Corning?

What's Romeo doing? Who is giving him orders? Who is still alive to run whatever plan is being played out? There aren't many suspects left.

And the most obvious is the one with the most power.

Harry. The now-president of the United States.

Was it Harry all along?

Now he's got Lily.

And it's all my fault.

The world goes grey, like a drawstring closing.

Blink.

. . .

GET the stunning conclusion of the False series in False Start, the final book in the False series by USA Today bestselling author Meli Raine.